WING OF THE DRAGON

MERCY VALLEY

BOOK ONE

TAILA CANTRELL

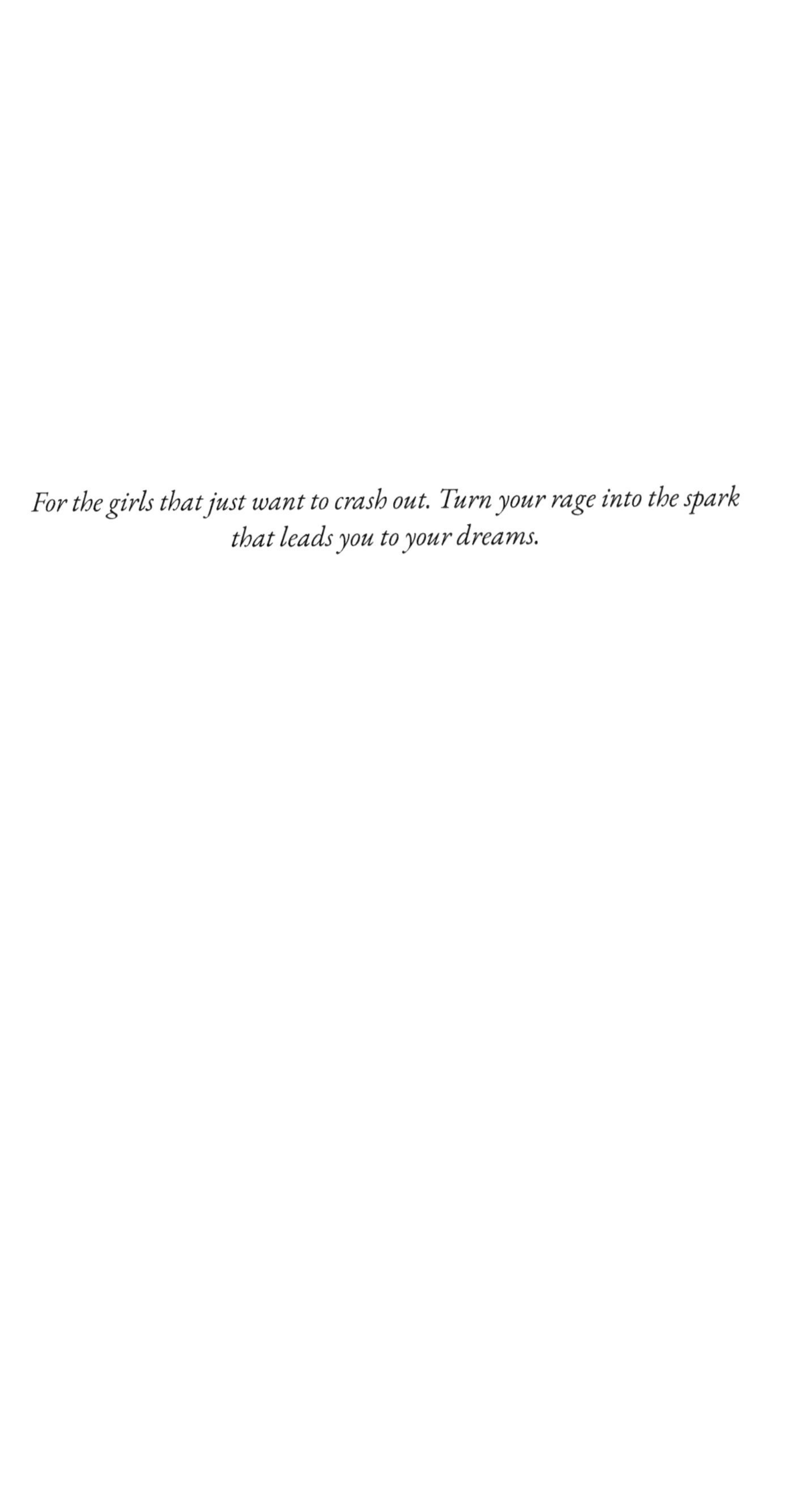

For the girls that just want to crash out. Turn your rage into the spark that leads you to your dreams.

WELCOME TO MERCY VALLEY

The mountains have always hidden secrets, but Mercy Valley's secrets are bigger than most.

Deep in the mountains of Tennessee, Mercy Valley welcomes its human tourists, but the people of the town? Shifters of all kinds, hidden in plain sight. From dragons in the sky to wolves roaming the woods, Mercy Valley is a safe haven for all shifters. But shifters aren't always an easy race, and when other supernaturals are involved... Well let's just say, it can get bloody.

Visit if you wish but know that danger can lurk around any corner.

Welcome To MERCY VALLEY
CORVID TERRITORY
DRAGON TERRITORY
LASER QUEST
MERCY VALLEY MOVIES
LASER QUEST
MAMA'S PEACE
BEE AND BEAR BOOKSTORE
STRONG ARM GYM
YELLER'S RESTURANT
JUNIPER'S FLOWERS
KRAKEN KUSH
EM'S BOUTIQUE
IZZY'S INTIMATES
CLUB SHIFT
DELCIOUS BEE'S
MERCY VALLEY POST OFFICE
ABE'S GROCERY
POST OFFICE
COYOTE TERRITORY
MERCY VALLEY PUBLIC LIBRARY
MERCY VALLEY POLICE STATION
MERCY VALLEY CEMETARY
WOLF TERRITORY
CAT TERRITORY
BEAR TERRITORY

I WAS DRUNK. I should have been hungover since it was eight o'clock in the morning, but I was still drunk as I stumbled up the steps into the mayor's mansion. I could barely get my keys in the door. My mother was going to kill me. I was supposed to be the picture of prim and proper. Instead, I was still dressed in the tiny, bright red dress I'd worn out to the club last night, only now I lacked panties. The guard at the gate, Caleb, I think, had let me in with a slight smirk. Pretty sure I saw him snap a picture when I'd bent down to retrieve my bag. I'm sure it would be all over Instagram later— just another thing for Mom to yell about later. It was my birthday, though, she'd forgive me. Even if my bare ass did go viral.

"Princess Fallon, where have you been?" Our butler, Mateo, shrieked as I pushed my way into the house.

"Shhh," I said, falling into his arms with a wince as I stumbled over the rug. "Horrible headache."

"You reek of alcohol." He growled, "Wait until your fathers..." His eyes turned sad, "Oh, Princess Fallon." Tears formed, and my instincts roared to life. Something was very wrong.

I straightened out of his arms, my beast taking over, clearing some of the haze from my mind. "Where is Mom? Or Papa and Dad?"

"There was a shooting..." Mateo trailed off, "Let me take you to the conference room. They've been looking for you."

My skin was clammy, my world off kilter. Something was horribly wrong, and my Dragon could smell death hanging in the air. I rushed toward the conference room, with Mateo hot on my heels. I burst through the doors, expecting to see my mother there leading the room as she always was. Instead, my fathers turned, their red and splotchy faces crumpling further as they took in my panting visage. "Fallon... come here, my baby," Dad said, wrapping me in his huge arms. "She's gone, Fal. Your momma has passed on."

Papa embraced Dad and I as a wail left my throat. I'd known, had known the moment I'd laid eyes on Mateo. The Clan was crumbling without my mother to rule over them. The Dragon Queen of the Occydent was dead. My mommy was gone, and with her death, every ounce of joy I'd ever felt seemed to sap away from me.

Our cries echoed through the house, and for a moment, I swore I could feel the pain of every Dragon in our Clan as we grieved the loss of Agana Eyre. She had ruled over the Dragons for two hundred years, had kept Mercy Valley safe for all the supernaturals. Her loss was too much. Who could fill the hole she had left in all of our hearts? I don't know how long my father's held me as we sobbed together. Eventually, we pulled apart, faces puffy and tear stained. Rage finally filled the space in my body, "What happened?"

"Agana was shot outside of Abe's Grocery. She had run out to grab some ice cream while we waited for you to get home. She insisted we stay here in case you came back or called." Papa explained.

"So, it's my fault?" My voice was small, horror filling me. She'd only been along because of me. If her mates had been with her, they could have protected her.

"No! You will not think that way. If they hadn't caught her out there, it would have happened when she was somewhere else." Dad snapped. Even though he said it, no part of me believed him. Because

I had decided to go out for my twenty-first birthday a little early, my mother was out late at night, alone, and she had been killed. "Don't worry, Fallon. We will hunt whoever did this. You only need to worry about preparing yourself for the throne."

"The throne." I parroted back.

"You'll have some time to grieve first, but Fallon, you are the next Dragon Queen of the Occydent. You will be expected to find your mates and take the throne." Papa said, placing his hands on my shoulders, "Agana has prepared you for this your entire life. You will be just fine."

"Queen." Was all I could say. The alcohol and emotions caught up to me all at once and I leaned over vomited on our shoes. I stood, swaying, seconds before I blacked out.

I was sick and fucking tired of sitting on this godforsaken chair. It was a torture device, metal and wood twisted high behind me, mimicking fire. Apparently, bringing a cushion to sit on was frowned upon. I still didn't understand how my mother had sat here for hours, looking completely comfortable. If this was what I had to look forward to as Queen, I needed to seriously consider running away while I still had the chance. Yet I stayed seated, back and ass aching, because it was what my mother would have done.

"Next will be Lord Gatlin Hambridge. He comes from good stock, though I've heard a rumor that his clan is fond of keeping indentured servants." Mateo whispered in my ear.

I nodded politely, keeping my commentary to myself. The man who entered the room barely reached my chest. He bowed before me, but something in his eyes was mocking as he approached. His scent reached my nose before he even opened his mouth. I had to stop myself from gagging at the sulfurous musk. I held up my hand, "Apologies, Lord Hambridge, but I can already tell you are not mated to me. The hour is getting late; would you be so kind as to allow me to retire early? I'm sure my father, Chaska, will be happy to discuss business dealings with you."

Lord Hambridge gritted his teeth so hard I could hear it, but he gave me a bright smile. "Princess Fallon, I appreciate your honesty. I would love to treat you to dinner tomorrow evening to make up for our lack of introduction. I'm sure that would be amenable to you."

I narrowed my eyes, but nodded, "That will be acceptable, Lord. You are dismissed."

He turned on his heel, exiting the room with some of his dignity back. "The Dabel precession will arrive tomorrow. You cannot treat the Prince of the Oryent with the same disregard you just showed Lord Hambridge." Dad said, stepping out of the shadows behind my throne. He'd lost weight, his clothes hanging off his large frame. It wouldn't be long before him, and Papa left me to return to my mother. I wasn't ready to lose my parents.

"I know the Prince is important. I will be on my best behavior." I said, giving him my most regal smile. The truth was, I didn't even believe that my mates were out there at this point. I was only twenty-one, and most dragons didn't meet their first mate until they were well into their fifties. It was unheard of for a Dragon Queen to take the throne under the age of one hundred. All of the Dragons that had flocked to our door the last few months were more interested in gawking at the young Dragon Princess than anything else. I was a pretty jewel on display. With each new male, my skin crawled, but I sat like a good little princess should. It was the least I could do for my fathers.

Dad sighed, "I know you hate this, Fallon. I had hoped you would find your mates organically, but this is a necessary evil. You cannot be alone when..." He trailed off, unable to speak of his and Papa's inevitable deaths. The fact that they had held on this long without their mate was a miracle, and a show of their deep love for me.

I stood, rushing into his waiting arms, "I'll be okay, Dad. I'm sure at least one of my mates will turn up soon." We embraced for a long time, before I finally pulled away. "I'm going to go up to my rooms for the night, I need to be prepared for the Prince's arrival tomorrow."

We said our goodbyes, and I quickly bounded up the stairs. I entered my room, stopping to lock my door before I turned to take in the space. It was messy since the shooting. Dad and Papa had sent most of our staff away. I was not a clean and organized person, so now my rooms always looked like a tiny tornado had been through them. Clothes were spread across the floor and half of the surfaces. My makeup table was covered in products, enough so you could barely see the marble top. I bypassed all of it, feeling only mildly guilty for letting it get this bad. I stepped into my closet, yanking the dark green dress I wore over my head. I grabbed black leggings and a black sweatshirt, yanking them on quickly.

In just a few minutes I would sneak off my balcony and into town. For months I had been quietly trying to gather evidence on who had killed my mother. I would find them, and my beast and I would deliver the justice that they deserved.

"*I don't sense anyone in the gardens below.*" My beast whispered into my mind as I gathered supplies. First, I yanked my deep red hair into a low bun, pulling on the blonde wig I'd purchased last month. I couldn't risk being recognized during my investigation. Huge black sunglasses went on next to cover my distinctive golden gaze. I slipped a wad of cash into my pocket, and a fake ID I had made just in case.

I glanced around the room one last time, promising myself that when I returned tonight, I would clean it. If Papa saw it in this state with the Prince's arrival tomorrow, he might have a coronary.

My beast slammed against the walls of my mind, "*Let us leave. I desire the hunt.*" My dragon grieved differently than I did. While I had cried and raged, she had laid in wait, itching for vengeance against whoever had taken her mother from her. It was difficult to control, but as a future Dragon Queen my control of my beast was ironclad.

With a deep breath, I called my wings. My clothes had been

enchanted by witches to adjust to whatever form I took, so the fabric parted with ease. I flapped the leathery appendages twice, before I stepped onto the rail of the balcony. I put my arms out before letting myself fall. My wings caught air easily, gliding on the wind. I flapped hard, aiming for the clouds that hung heavy over the late day sun. Once I was sure I would not be seen I aimed for town. Tonight, I was sure I would find something that would change the tides of my search for revenge. I had to.

MERCY VALLEY WAS a beautiful small town, nestled deep in the Appalachian Mountains of East Tennessee. It held a charm that could not be ignored. Yet the secrets the town held were far more interesting. Shifters had created this town as a safe haven hundreds of years ago. No matter what animal you shifted into, you would find a home in Mercy Valley. I wished I could appreciate it with the same eyes that the human tourists did. Instead, I saw the darkness that lurked in the corners. The bloody fights for territory between the wolves and the coyotes, the vampires who lurked in the night waiting for their prey, the unsettled ghosts seeking their vengeance in the afterlife, uncovened witches hiding from their people. I may have loved my town, but it was not a perfect utopia. Mom had been working to change that. She had facilitated peace between the cat shifters and the wolves, had given the corvids land. She had worked her entire life for the shifters of Mercy Valley. Yet someone had murdered her for all her trouble. I couldn't wrap my mind around why. Sure, there had been the occasional threat. We were beasts after all, when our blood ran hot, things were said. But for someone to shoot her three times in cold blood... It made no sense. Shifters settled their grievances with claws and teeth, not guns.

"ID." The bouncer of the club looked me over with a sneer. I wasn't dressed well enough to be here, but I couldn't bring myself to care. I didn't really want to visit Club Shift. I hadn't since the night my mother was murdered, but every lead I found brought me back to the owner. Cecil Vaegra, a vampire of means. He wasn't often in town, but he was this week.

I slipped inside, ignoring the bright lights and music. The dancers on the dance floor made me snarl. How could these people be so carefree while my mother was dead? I took a deep breath, shaking my head. My beast was too close to the surface.

I watched the crowds for a long time, getting my mind in order. I couldn't approach Cecil if I wasn't in control. When I finally decided I was calm enough I made my way to the stairs into the VIP area. No guard waited to stop me, so I followed my nose to the scent of blood. As I got closer, I heard voices in the office. I stayed in the shadows, listening to the conversation.

"The Dragons of the Occident are weak right now." I froze at those words. I had no doubt the person speaking was Cecil, with his strange, ancient accent.

"Maybe, but if I would not underestimate them either. Whoever killed Agana Eyre will suffer."

The voice that responded was smooth with no accent, but it held a quality that sent shivers down my spine. "Consider my offer, Cecil. I think we could help each other. Wouldn't it be nice to be out from under the thumb of Dragons?"

Whatever else was said between the men was lost to me as a scent so mouthwatering I nearly stepped out of my hiding place drifted to my nose. My beast reacted, a growled, *"Mate."* filled my mind. Panic clawed at my throat; there was no chance any mate of mine had dealings with this vampire. Not a future King. I was frozen. The scent of ginger and orchids grew stronger as the sound of steps came closer to my hiding place. I hadn't put on my scent dampening perfume before I left. I was stupid, and as the man appeared before my hiding place my body began to shake. From his profile I could tell he was of Asian descent, his black hair brushed his shoulders as he took a deep breath. He wore black jeans and a blood red button down. I could tell the moment he caught my scent because he froze, his nose sniffing the air. He whirled toward me, but I was already moving. I slid past him, running down the stairs and through the club as his roar followed me. I slipped into a dark alley, unfurling my wings and taking to the sky as quickly as I could.

Fear slowly crept up my spine. I was mated to a man that was trying to work with Cecel Vaegra. The man who quite possibly killed my mother. My beast tried to make it reasonable, *"If our mate wants to work with him that proves his innocence."*

I landed on my balcony with a heavy thud. My emotions were cloudy as I collapsed onto the bed. I had to sleep and get myself together. I had to meet the son the Dragon Queen of the Oryent in the morning. I couldn't tell anyone I'd met one of my mates.

"Princess Fallon!" I cringed at Lord Hambridge's voice carried down the hallway. I was hoping to avoid his breakfast plans, but I'd had no such luck. My skin crawled as he rushed to my side, "I'm so glad I caught you. Please join me for breakfast in my room." I opened my mouth to deny his invitation, but he cut me off, "I understand your hesitancy. I am not your mate, so I'm sure you feel that I have nothing I could offer. If you would just sit down with me, I believe we can help each out."

I held in the sigh. He was certainly tenacious, "Alright Lord Hambridge. Lead the way."

I followed the stout man to his rooms. Mateo stepped out, carrying an empty tray, "Lord Hambridge, I've placed your breakfast on the balcony. Your... assistant insisted that I leave so that he could serve you."

Mateo's eyes drifted to me, giving me a meaningful look. The rumors of Lord Hambridge's assistants must be true if that was how he felt. "Thank you, Mateo." I said when Lord Hambridge ignored him.

I didn't like the man, and I wasn't sure there was any reason to waste my time meeting with him. At least if I had a meal with him maybe he would leave me alone.

"Abasom, serve the Princess first." Lord Hambridge snapped as I stepped out onto the balcony. I looked up, before my body froze.

A giant stood next to Lord Hambridge's chair. The man was easily pushing seven feet tall. Dragons were large, but he put all of the men I knew to shame. His dark hair was buzzed short, tattoos were visible on his neck and forearms. His eyes were downcast as he shuffled around the table, pulling out a chair for me. To see a man like this in the role of a servant set my beast off, *"That is a King among Dragons. Why does he behave as a slave?"*

"Lord Hambridge is known for having indentured servants, usually due to debts owed to him by clan members." I explained as I took my seat.

"Burn him. No Dragon should ever serve a man so weak." My beast growled, but I pushed her away, focusing on Lord Hambridge as he continued to speak regardless of my lack of response.

"I hope you won't be offended by what I'm about to say Princess. You seem like a very reasonable woman. With your age you are going to need people on your side. People with power who can advise you on all matters of things your mother may not have had the chance to teach you." He said.

I stiffened, reading between the lines. "I'm sure my mates will make excellent advisors. After all isn't that why we believe the Queen to be blessed with multiple?" He opened his mouth to respond, but I continued, "Thank God, my mother worked so hard to teach me all that she knew at such a young age."

"Indeed." He said, glancing to his servant, "You see Princess. I worry that your mother may have put certain ideas into your head that would not be best for the Dragons of the Occident to continue."

I narrowed my eyes, "Like what?"

Before he could respond his servant leaned into my space to pour my cup of tea and I caught his scent. Pine trees and something darker that I couldn't describe reached my nose. I stood, causing my chair to tumble backwards. "You're my mate." I blurted down at the giant.

He finally met my eyes, giving me a look at the pale blue irises he'd been hiding. He flared his nostrils catching my scent. With a growl I was snatched into his arms as he launched his body over the balcony. A scream ripped from my throat before his deep black wings unfurled. He flapped quickly, zooming away from my home. I studied his wings, unable to think of anything but his hot body pressed against mine. There were deep scars along the ridges of his wings. They reminded me of whips marks I'd seen in history books from when humans kept dragons as pets. I cringed, realizing just how complicated our situation had just become.

Eventually, he landed in the forest a couple of miles away, but he didn't sit me down. Instead, he paced with my body flung over his shoulders. Growls left him, but no words. With a deep breath I quietly said, "Abasom, can you at least put me down?"

He growled, "Don't call me that." Though he did honor my request and sit me on my feet. I stared up at him, waiting for him to say something else. We took each other in for a long moment, "Your eyes are beautiful." He whispered.

"Thank you. You are very strong." The exchange was awkward. It lacked real flirtation, "What do you want me to call you."

"Mate." He responded. I bit my tongue to stop myself from laughing. I'm sure he would be offended. When he saw the look on my face his cheeks turned bright pink. An odd look for the large man, "My name is Bain."

"It's nice to meet you, Bain. I'm Fallon." I said, offering him my hand.

He stared for a long moment, "I know who you are. The Dragon Queen of the Occident."

"Not yet." I pointed out, "Right now I am just Princess Fallon."

He cringed at the reminder. Something dark filled his eyes, "I cannot be your mate."

The rejection was casual, but it cut me deeply. A mate denying the bond was unheard of, especially for the Dragons Queens. As I watched him, the scars that lined his wings, the set of his powerful shoulders in defeat I realized something. "You fear Hambridge."

"He is my Master." Bain gritted out. The submission didn't suit him. This was a man who was made to dominant. Yet his eyes were downcast.

"I will remove his head." That words that left my mouth weren't all mine. My beast pushing to the surface desperate to be closer to her mate. I agreed with her. If Hambridge was the reason for my mate's unnatural disposition, for the scars that lined his wings we would execute him as soon as we returned.

"I am a servant to the Hambridge clan. I cannot be released from my oath to him. Even if he dies my oath will simply pass to his heir." Bain explained, though speaking seemed to be painful for him.

"I will find a way." I argued. My mate would not be a servant to anyone. It was a disgrace to his position.

He looked at me, but no hope filled his eyes, "I should not have stolen you away."

I glanced up at the sun that had begun to climb higher in the sky, "I need to return. I have to meet the Dragon Prince of the Orient soon..." I trailed off. I didn't want to. I knew just how awful the spoiled royals of shifters could be. Meeting the Prince of the Orient was a formality. To ensure that the Dragon Queen of the Orient's only unmated son wasn't my mate.

"I am sorry, Princess." He said. His wings drooped slightly as he turned away from me.

"Would you like to fly together?" I blurted out.

Some small joy lit in his eyes. He nodded, so I produced my wings. Unlike his deep black, mine were a mix of gold and red. He admired them for a long moment, before reaching out to run a finger down one of the ridges. I hissed through my teeth, unable to hide the shiver of pleasure that ran down my spine. He smirked, but flapped his wings as he bent in knees, shooting into the sky with little effort. I mirrored his action until I fluttered beside him.

We flew together, circling and diving until we were both laughing. It was the lightest I'd seen him in the short time we'd had together. As we got closer to the manner, I led him to my balcony. Once we landed I opened my "Princess Fallon!" I cringed at Lord Hambridge's voice carried down the hallway. I was hoping to avoid his meal plans, but I'd had no such luck. My skin crawled as he rushed to my side, "I'm so glad I caught you. Please join me for breakfast in my room." I opened my mouth to deny his invitation, but he cut me off, "I understand your hesitancy. I am not your mate, so I'm sure you feel that I have nothing I could offer. If you would just sit down with me, I believe we can help each other out."

I held in the sigh. He was certainly tenacious, "Alright, Lord Hambridge. Lead the way."

I followed the stout man to his rooms. Mateo stepped out, carrying an empty tray. "Lord Hambridge, I've placed your breakfast on the balcony. Your... assistant insisted that I leave so that he could serve you."

Mateo's eyes drifted to me, giving me a meaningful look. The rumors of Lord Hambridge's assistants must be true if that was how he felt. "Thank you, Mateo," I said when Lord Hambridge ignored him. I didn't like the man, and I wasn't sure there was any reason to waste my time meeting with him. At least if I had a meal with him, maybe he would leave me alone.

"Abasom, serve the Princess first." Lord Hambridge snapped as I stepped out onto the balcony. I looked up, before my body froze.

A giant stood next to Lord Hambridge's chair. The man was easily seven feet tall. Dragons were large, but he put all of the men I knew to shame. His dark hair was buzzed short, and scars were visible on his neck and forearms. His eyes were downcast as he shuffled around the table, pulling out a chair for me. To see a man like this in the role of a servant set my beast off, *That is a King among Dragons. Why does he behave as a slave?*

"Lord Hambridge is known for having indentured servants,

usually due to debts owed to him by clan members," I explained as I took my seat.

"Burn him. No Dragon should ever serve a man so weak." My beast growled, but I pushed her away, focusing on Lord Hambridge as he continued to speak regardless of my lack of response.

"I hope you won't be offended by what I'm about to say, Princess. You seem like a very reasonable woman. With your age, you will need people on your side. People with power who can advise you on all matters of things your mother may not have had the chance to teach you." He said.

I stiffened, reading between the lines. "I'm sure my mates will make excellent advisors. After all isn't that why we believe the Queen to be blessed with multiple?" He opened his mouth to respond, but I continued. "Thank God, my mother worked so hard to teach me all that she knew at such a young age."

"Indeed." He said, glancing to his servant, "You see Princess. I worry that your mother may have put certain ideas into your head that would not be best for the Dragons of the Occydent to continue."

I narrowed my eyes, "Like what?"

Before he could respond his servant leaned into my space to pour my cup of tea and I caught his scent. Pine trees and something darker that I couldn't describe reached my nose. I stood, causing my chair to tumble backwards. "You're my mate." I blurted down at the giant. My beast pressed to the surface, hunger driving her to push closer to our mate. I held myself back, watching the man carefully.

He finally met my eyes, giving me a look at the pale blue irises he'd been hiding. He flared his nostrils catching my scent. With a growl I was snatched into his arms as he launched his body over the balcony. A scream ripped from my throat before his deep black wings unfurled. He flapped quickly, zooming away from my home. I studied his wings, unable to think of anything but his hot body pressed against mine. There were deep scars along the ridges of his wings. They reminded me of whips marks I'd seen in history books from when humans kept dragons as pets. I cringed, realizing just how complicated our situation had just become. Eventually, he landed in the forest a couple of miles away, but he didn't sit me down. Instead, he paced with my body flung over his shoulders. Growls left him, but no words. With a deep breath I quietly said, "Abasom, can you at least put me down?"

He growled, "Don't call me that." Though he did honor my request and sat me on my feet. I stared up at him, waiting for him to say something else. We took each other in for a long moment, "Your eyes are beautiful." He whispered.

"Thank you. You are very strong." The exchange was awkward. It lacked real flirtation, "What do you want me to call you?"

"Mate." He responded. I bit my tongue to stop myself from laughing. I'm sure he would be offended. When he saw the look on my face his cheeks turned bright pink. An odd look for the large man, "My name is Bain."

"It's nice to meet you, Bain. I'm Fallon." I said, offering him my hand.

He stared for a long moment, "I know who you are. The Dragon Queen of the Occydent."

"Not yet." I pointed out, "Right now I am just Princess Fallon."

He cringed at the reminder. Something dark filled his eyes, "I cannot be your mate."

The rejection was casual, but it cut me deeply. A mate denying the bond was unheard of, especially for the Dragons Queens. As I watched him, the scars that lined his wings, the set of his powerful shoulders in defeat I realized something. "You fear Hambridge."

"He is my Master." Bain gritted out. The submission didn't suit him. This was a man who was made to dominant. Yet his eyes were downcast.

"I will remove his head." That words that left my mouth weren't all mine. My beast pushing to the surface desperate to be closer to her mate. I agreed with her. If Hambridge was the reason for my mate's unnatural disposition, for the scars that lined his wings we would execute him as soon as we returned.

"I am a servant to the Hambridge clan. I cannot be released from my oath to him. Even if he dies my oath will simply pass to his heir." Bain explained, though speaking seemed to be painful for him.

"I will find a way." I argued. My mate would not be a servant to anyone. It was a disgrace to his position.

He looked at me, but no hope filled his eyes, "I should not have stolen you away."

I glanced up at the sun that had begun to climb higher in the sky, "I need to return. I have to meet the Dragon Prince of the Oryent soon..." I trailed off. I didn't want to. I knew just how awful the spoiled royals of shifters could be. Meeting the Prince of the Oryent was a formality. To ensure that the Dragon Queen of the Oryent's only unmated son wasn't my mate.

"I am sorry, Princess." He said. His wings drooped slightly as he turned away from me.

"Would you like to fly together?" I blurted out.

Some small joy lit in his eyes. He nodded, so I produced my wings. Unlike his deep black, mine were blood red, nearly the same color as my hair. He admired them for a long moment, before reaching out to run a finger down one of the ridges. I hissed through my teeth, unable to hide the shiver of pleasure that ran down my spine. He smirked, but flapped his wings as he bent his knees, shooting into the sky with little effort. I mirrored his action until I fluttered beside him. We flew together, circling and diving until we were both laughing. It was the lightest I'd seen him in the short time we'd had together. As we got closer to the manner, I led him to my balcony. Once we landed, I opened my mouth, but he didn't give me a chance to speak. His lips crashed into mine, claiming me with tongue and teeth. I melted into his body, desperate to be closer to him.

He pulled away, opening the door to my bedroom. As soon as I stepped inside, I rushed to push him back out, "No, my rooms are a mess. You can't see them. You'll think I'm a spoiled slob." My sitting room wasn't quite as destroyed as my bedroom and bathroom, but that didn't mean I wanted him to see any of it.

He grunted, moving past me. He took the room in with a critical eye, causing me to shift from foot to foot in embarrassment. "I will clean them."

"N-no you can't." I rushed to say. It was not his job to serve me. I should have cleaned my own rooms last night.

"Go meet the Prince. When you return your rooms will be clean." He commanded, "I will have to return to Lord Hambridge. I am sorry I cannot be the mate you deserve. At least allow me to take this burden from you."

I couldn't argue with him. While he may not see a way out of whatever oath he'd sworn to Hambridge, I was the future goddamn Queen. Hambridge would bow before me and release my mate from his servitude. I just needed to talk to Papa and Dad. I sighed, "Okay."

"You will find other mates more deserving of you, Princess." He said, before escorting me to the hallway.

I stood on my tiptoes pressing a kiss to his cheek before I headed down to the throne room. When I entered the room was in chaos. Mateo, Dad, and Papa stood at the throne, several people crowded in front of them, shouting incoherently. As I approached every eye turned to me, silence filling the cavernous space. Papa approached, his golden eyes so like mine simmering with rage, "Where have you been?" He hissed in a whisper.

"I met one of my mates. There are... complications. We will discuss it later." I rushed to explain careful to keep my voice low. Dragons had better hearing than most humans, but I hoped to keep the information private for now. His eyes widened, and he nodded before escorting me to the throne. Before I sat, I said, "My apologies for my tardiness. There was a matter of utmost importance I had to attend to. I will extend my apologies to the Prince directly as soon as he arrives."

I received a couple of glares from the Prince's escorts, but most of the gazes and murmurs were understandable. A woman with gorgeous, sleek black hair stepped forward. "Introducing Prince Archer Dabel, seventh son of the Queen Phaedra of the Orient." Her voice echoed, as the doors opened.

I kept my face neutral as the man stepped through the doors, but when his nose flared and he flew toward me I had to hold back a terrified squeak. His blazing red eyes narrowed as he said, "You look far nicer with red hair than blonde, mate."

With those words, the room descended back into chaos. I did nothing, staring up at the man that had been meeting with Cecil Vaegra last night. What business would the Prince of the Oryent have with the vampire? And what exactly did he offer Cecil? Secrets piled up at every corner with both of my mates. None of this was going to be simple.

"This is wonderful, Fallon. I don't understand why you're upset. You've found two of your mates after months of failure!" Dad said, pacing in front of me. We had retired to his study to discuss our situation.

The beautiful escort of Prince Archer had dragged him from the room after his outburst. Whether we were mated or not, it was not a good look. "I want to know what the Prince meant," Papa added in from his seat behind the desk.

I stared at the ceiling from my place on the chaise lounge. I didn't want to tell them the truth about last night. It would only worry them, but I couldn't pretend I didn't know what he was talking about. I sighed. I didn't have any choice. "I went out to Club Shifter last night." They both gasped and began talking, but I held my hand up, "I was in disguise. I've been... hunting Mom's killer for months. A lead led me there."

"The Prince was there?" Dad said.

"That's the first thing you're going to ask?" Papa snapped, "Our daughter snuck out in the middle of the night, to the most dangerous place in town."

Dad sighed, "She's a grown woman, Wendel. She's just a short few months from being the Queen. We cannot protect her from life. That isn't what Agana would want." Papa threw his hands in the air, clearly unable to argue with Dad. Dad turned to me, "What has you so bothered, Fallon? It's not just that you ran into the Prince last night. You said you met another mate. Where is he?"

I flinched, "You're really not going to like this."

"Apparently, that's the story of my day." Papa chimed in, "What's going on, my flower. Let us help you."

"My other mate is Lord Hambridge's servant. He says his oath cannot be broken." Both of their faces crumbled. "And I overheard a conversation between the Prince Archer and Cecil Vaegra that was... concerning, to say the least."

"Fuck." Papa slammed his hands down on the desk as smoke drifted from his nose. "We can't do much about the Prince. You're going to have to find out more about what he was doing there without making accusations that could plunge us into a war."

"I know. Honestly, Bain is more important to me right now." I admitted. Archer was a problem but his title made the situation too complicated to address. I would find out what he was doing there, it was just going to take time.

Dad hummed softly, "Lord Hambridge's Clan has been known for his oaths and servants for hundreds of years. I'll have to do some research, but surely he can see the value of having a member of his Clan on the throne."

"I hate that man." Papa said.

"He's fucking insufferable." I pointed out, "Can't I just kill him?"

"Fallon!" Papa gasped. "Blood thirst is understandable in the situation, but you cannot just casually discuss killing a Lord."

"It's for my mate." I growled. My beast was unsettled, and if I didn't shift soon it was going to become a problem.

Papa and I were always like this. I took after him the most, our tempers would flare anytime we didn't agree on something. Usually,

Mom's quiet dominance had prevented our back and forths from becoming violent. Dad stepped in before it could escalate further, "Fallon, your eyes are glowing. Go take care of your needs. We will do some research and try to talk Hambridge. I also have to go smooth things over with Duchess Honora. She might have drug the Prince from the room, but I could see the calculations in her eyes. If she thinks she can turn your mating into a political scandal of some kind, she's got another thing coming."

I left the room shortly after, unable to take another moment of sitting and discussing the situations. I needed to take action, but first I needed to get out of this dress.

As I stepped into my room I gasped. Every surface was clean and sparkly. My make up table had been neatly organized. There was no sign of the chaos that had been there when I'd left this morning. The act of service made my heart flutter. This was the behavior of a mate, lightening the burden. As I approached my perfectly made bed, I noticed a note and something wrapped in a black, silk cloth. I read the note first.

"Princess Fallon,

I hope you find the room to your expectations. I also took the liberty of washing and putting away your laundry.

I will be urging Lord Hambridge to leave today. You deserve a better mate. I will not do you the dishonor of a formal rejection

I left you a small gift so that you may always carry a piece of me with you."

I dropped the note, reaching for the small black cloth. I unfolded it carefully, revealing a tiny golden ring. Clearly, it would have been too small for my giant mate, but it slipped perfectly onto my pinky finger. Emotions warred inside of me. My beast took the opportunity to rise to the front of my mind, my lungs constricted, fire begging to be released. I slipped into the back of my mind, letting my beast take over. I watched as she stormed from our bedroom, arriving before Lord Hambridge's door in seconds. She pounded on the door, and I could see the red scales that shimmered along my arms. When Hambridge's face appeared before me, my dragon grabbed his thick neck, lifting him off the ground without a word. She was beyond speaking as she pushed into the room.

Bain appeared from an adjoining room, his blue eyes widening at the scene. "Princess, put down my Lord."

My dragon took in our mate's scent, nearly salivating, "I've come to remove his head." She responded. I could feel the grin splitting across my face, "You belong to me and me alone." She declared, turning her attention back to Hambridge. His face was turning purple, and I took note that his brown wings had been released. His shifted claws fought against our hold, but he was no match for a pissed off royal. My beast was one of the strongest of our kind, a Royal Dragon in a rage over their mate was a danger very few survived. "Would you prefer I roast him alive or decapitate him so that all our enemies may see his head on a spike outside?" The casual tone of her question didn't fit the rage I still felt simmering in my body. My chest was constricted from our fire building. I would burn out soon if my beast didn't release it.

Bain's eyes were darker as he approached, and my beast recognized that his beast was present. She turned to him fully, still maintaining her grasp on the Lord, "Welcome, mate. It is time for our vengeance."

He growled. The sound vibrated through us, "Put. Him. Down."

My beast narrowed her eyes. She spoke to me, *"Why does he defend this pathetic creature?"*

"He is his servant. He is honor bound to protect him from harm." I explained, realizing just how badly I had lost control. *"Release him. Let me take over."*

"No." With that she pulled from me. I attempted to take control of our body back, but she pushed me away easily. "You wish to stay bound to him?" My beast asked Bain.

His jaw clenched, the blues of his eyes glowing brighter, "Wishes do not matter. He is my master. You disrespect me by harming him."

My dragon did not like this at all. Her reaction was equivalent to an enraged toddler, but far more deadly as smoke began to pour from my nose. Her foot stomped down, "You would reject me for this?" Lord Hambridge was not prepared as my beast slammed him into the ground, releasing his neck as she placed our heeled foot on his chest. "You would choose weakness?" She ground our heel down, causing Lord Hambridge to scream.

"I have no choice." Bain responded.

My beast scoffed, "You are a Dragon, destined to be a King. There was always a choice."

Bain moved closer, panting, energy swirling around us as Hambridge cried out below. Just before Bain would have touched me my fathers appeared in the doorway, taking in the scene.

"Fallon." Dad's voice distracted my dragon. She recognized our fathers, and it brought pain to her that we would soon lose them. "Fallon Take back control. There are other ways to handle this."

Papa moved toward us, his hands held out, "Come, little love. Let us handle this situation. You can go fly, hunt. We will take care of your mate." He spoke directly to my beast, the nickname reserved for her alone.

Bain had stepped away, returning to his usual posture. Eyes downcast, shoulders slumped. I could see the tension in his body. Tension that I had created. My beast might have made his life much worse with her actions. I pushed forward, caressing my beast in my mind, lulling her back in her cage to rest. My vision cleared, the fire threatening to be released at any moment dissipated in an instant, causing me to stumble backward. Lord Hambridge wailed, but I ignored him. Glancing to Bain I gave him a nod, bringing his attention to the ring on my finger. His eyes finally met mine, and the pain that laid there nearly had me losing control again. Instead, I leaned down, helping Hambridge to his feet, "My apologies, Lord Hambridge. It seems my beast has made a grievous error. The emotions of finding two mates in one day must have overwhelmed my senses. Please, speak with my fathers. I am sure there is some way we can make it up to you."

He opened his mouth to speak, but his voice was only a squeak. Deep bruises in the same of my fingers lined his neck. I found satisfaction in the marks, but kept my face apologetic. "This was not the behavior of a Queen!" Hambridge announced loudly, "That you'd even consider mating a servant of Clan Hambridge is... is..." He trailed off at the growls my fathers both let loose.

"Careful how you speak to my daughter, Gatlin. We are still the Kings of the Occydent." Dad said, stepping forward, "A mate of any rank from Clan Hambridge is an honor to you. I'm sure we can discuss the matter over drinks."

Hambridge paled at the threat, but I saw the spark in his eyes at the idea of drinks with the Kings. He would find a way to turn my being mated to Bain to his advantage. The man wanted nothing but power. "Yes, well. I'm sure we can come to an amenable agreement for all." He said, straightening his spine.

I gave a small curtsy before I took my leave without a glance to anyone else. As I got closer to my rooms the feeling of being watched caused the hairs on my body to stand on end. I got the scent of ginger and orchids, and whirled around. "Lurking in the shadows doesn't fit the reputation of the Prince of the Oryent well."

Archer Dabel stepped out from the small alcove just a few feet from my room. "Just taking a note from your playbook, Princess."

My cheeks flamed at the reminder of our run in at Club Shifter, "What do you want?"

"Can a man not want to talk to his newly discovered mate?" He shot back. His red eyes bore into me. I wondered what he saw, what he had heard standing out here. The exchange in Lord's Hambridge's room had not been quiet. I stood in silence, forcing him to speak first, "We have a duty to our people, Princess."

I snorted, "Interesting for you to speak of duty." The man who had a meeting with Cecil Vaegra, who had allowed the vampire to call the Dragons of the Occydent weak. I still didn't know what he was doing there, what he may have offered Cecil.

Archer stepped into my personal space, "My mother will be flying in in thirty days. She will expect us to be ready for our mating ceremony when she arrives. Our secrets aside, we must begin to court."

My mouth went dry at the idea of meeting the Dragon Queen of the Oryent. She was legendary, pushing nearly five hundred years old. She had sixteen hatchlings, and only the man before me remained unmated. Her dynasty was secure. Meanwhile, my mother was dead, my fathers were dying, and both of my mates were... complicated. I could not allow her to come here and think that the Dragons of the Occydent were weak, but I didn't trust Archer. He was hiding things. Things I feared would harm my people if he was on the throne. "I will be at your door at eleven am sharp for our first breakfast together. Wear something nice." He commanded, before striding away without my response.

I slipped into my room, mind spinning. I had planned to return to Club Shifter tonight, but I was too exhausted and out of control to risk it. I laid on my bed, grabbing my forgotten cell phone from the bedside table. Bain must have found it and charged it. I didn't have many friends, so there were no notifications. I opened the photos app, scrolling through pictures of my life before my mother had been killed. Things had been simple then. I hadn't been worried about ruling, mates, or anything but having fun. I was the only hatchling my parents had, and they had certainly spoiled me greatly. Sure, Mom had been teaching me things about ruling since I was old enough to talk, but it had always been a distant future. Tears ran down my face. I needed to find her killer, but my duties as the soon to be Queen were becoming more demanding.

I switched over to my contacts, hovering over a name I hadn't thought of in years. With a deep breath I dialed the number. It was answered on the second ring, "What do you want?"

"It's time I call in my favor. You know where I live, be here soon." I demanded before hanging up. I dropped my phone back on the nightstand, looking out at the sun that now hung low in the sky. Another day wasted without any answer for who killed my mother. It didn't matter that I had found my mates. They would be no help in my greatest task right now.

I was pulling on my boots when the knock echoed at my door. Archer was punctual if nothing else. I stood, glancing at myself in the mirror. I'd pulled on black jeans and a green silk blouse, finishing the look off with knee-high leather boots. The only jewelry I wore was the small golden ring Bain had left for me. I couldn't bring myself to take it off.

Another insistent knock had me throwing open my bedroom door with a flourish. "Good morning, Prince."

"Good morning, Princess. You look delectable," Archer responded, his eyes roving over my body. "Accompany me to brunch in town?"

"As if I have a choice," I responded with a bright smile. I might not like it, but there was no getting rid of Prince Archer Dabel. In a month, we would be mated until one of us died. I just hoped I could uncover his secrets before then.

"Duty over desire." Archer responded as we made our way out of the mansion, "That is my mother's catchphrase. She made sure all of her hatchlings were aware that their desires meant nothing in the face of their duties to the crown."

I didn't respond at first, mulling over what he had said. "My mother cared more about my happiness than knowing I'd be Queen one day. She had faith that all that she had taught me would be enough."

Archer didn't respond as he opened the car door. I knew a bullet-proof vehicle when I saw one, so I slid into the sports car without a second thought. Wherever he'd managed to get this from, I was impressed. He slid into the driver's seat. "Our mothers may not have handled their hatchlings the same, but they were good friends. I hope their friendship will help your concerns with our mating."

"I have no issues with your mother." I'd never met Queen Phaedra formally, though I had walked in on a few phone calls between her and my mother over the years. She struck me as a very stern woman.

"But you have an issue with me?" He asked. I let the purr of the engine lull me as he flew around the curves that led into the main town of Mercy Valley.

"I don't trust anyone that would meet with Cecil Vaegra in the middle of the night." I said, trying to keep my voice light. I knew I was failing, because my beast stirred at my emotions.

Archer sighed, but didn't respond at first. I took in his profile, the long lashes that protected his glaring red eyes, the slope of his nose, full lips. The man look like he belonged in a kpop band. The girls would be desperate for him. I wondered if he could sing. "I just wanted information from him."

"What kind of information?" I asked.

"The kind that isn't for spoiled little princesses." He growled back.

Fire burned in my chest, "How fucking dare you!" I roared, "You come to my city, and claim that information you're looking for isn't my business. I will be Queen soon. Everything in Mercy Valley is my business."

His knuckles were white on the steering wheel as he glared at me. I refused to break eye contact. Eventually, he cursed, turning his eyes back to the road as we got closer to town. I smirked, knowing I had won this round… yet that victory was hollow. I still had no real answers to what the Prince was up to. He slid into a free parking space at the only diner in town, Mama's Place. The bear shifters had opened it years before I had been born in honor of their mother's love of cooking. It was one of the most popular places in town, the food was absolutely mouthwatering.

We walked inside together. A few shifters glanced our way, scenting us, but they turned back to their food without acknowledgement. I hadn't truly been part of the Mercy Valley community since just after my eighteenth birthday. I cringed as I thought about the incident, forcing my thoughts away from it.

"Welcome in, Princess," A smiling, older woman said, "Would you like a more private table?" From her scent I could tell she was part of the bear shifter's clan, but I couldn't pinpoint anything else.

"Yes, please." The Prince answered for me, causing me to stiffen.

She escorted us through the busy restaurant, leading us through a doorway in the back. The room was virtually empty aside from a few members of the staff. We took our seats at a booth, and I noted the claws mark dug into the edge of the table. "We use this space when there's small squabbles between the different shifters or when we have guests that may want their conversations to be private. My name is Hannah; I'll be the one to serve you today. Here's the menu. Our special today is locally caught rainbow trout. I'll give you both a few minutes to decide on what you'd like." She shooed the couple of straggling staff away, leaving Archer and I alone again.

I looked over the menu as if I was unsure what I would order. I always got the same thing, a rare ribeye with the garlic mashed potatoes and green beans. It had been my favorite meal to order when Mom, Dad, and Papa would bring me here. I kept my eyes on the menu, avoiding eye contact with Archer. His scent was somehow stronger now than it had been in the car, and my beast was glancing through my eyes with curiosity. *"He's a powerful Dragon, a very worthy mate for us."*

"Maybe so, but he's dishonest. And I did a little digging last night; he's got a reputation for sleeping around." I pointed out.

"I'll eat anyone he thinks to look at for too long." My beast responded, before returning to her usual resting place. I wasn't actually worried about Archer sleeping with other women. Once a Dragon was mated, the option of sleeping with anyone else went away. Our Dragons couldn't... function with other partners once our mates had been found.

"Listen Fallon-" Archer started, but Hannah returned asking, "What did y'all decide on?"

"I'll take the rare ribeye, garlic mashed potatoes and green beans. Just a water to drink, but bring me a chocolate malt later?" I ordered.

Hannah grinned, "Absolutely. The chocolate malt is my favorite as well. And for you sir?"

"I'll have the same, minus the malt." Archer said.

"Sounds good. I'll have that out to you shortly." Hannah said before leaving us alone once again.

"Fallon"

"Archer," I snapped my mouth closed, giving him the chance to speak.

"I can see that we've started off on the wrong foot. I don't want our mating to be one of discontent. We both know that we owe it to our clans to mate and provide strong heirs to rule." I cringed at the mention of heirs, but he continued. "I hope you can come to understand that while there may be secrets between us, we can still present a strong front for our people."

"Oh." The word spilled out against my will. I was disappointed that Archer didn't see that his secrets should not be more important than our mate bond. "I will... Keep that in mind."

He nodded at my response, letting silence fill the room. If I couldn't find a way to change the direction of my relationship with my mates, I would be ruling the Dragons of the Occydent alone. Archer would only consider duty; his rigid stance now led me to believe there was no changing his mind. Meanwhile, Bain seemed content to stay a servant to Lord Hambridge. I would be the only Royal that truly cared for my people with no support like my Dad and Papa. Horror struck me as I realized that even choosing to have a hatchling would be out of duty.

I stood from the table suddenly, "I... have to go to the restroom."

Archer raised an eyebrow but didn't comment as I rushed out of the room. There was nothing I could do as the first tear fell down my cheek. Instead of going to the bathroom, I ended up outside, hiding in the alley. A door swung open causing me to flinch. When a huge burly man stepped outside, lighting a cigarette I relaxed. He glanced toward me, seeing my tear stricken face. Instead of speaking he pulled out his pack of cigarettes and offered me one. I didn't hesitate to take one, allowing him to light it for me. The first drag calmed my nerves, the second released the tension in my muscles.

"You good?" The man rumbled. I glanced up, realizing he was one of the sons of the bear shifter's leader. I nodded, "Elex. You got a problem, let me know and I'll handle it."

"Fallon. I've just got mate issues." I sighed. Elex grumbled in response. We smoked in silence.

"I don't know how Dragons treat their women, but if you've got mate issues... It's not your job to fix them. They should be trying to impress you, not the other way around." I raised my eyebrows at the wise words. The bear didn't seem talkative, so his words meant more.

"Lay off the cigs before you meet your mate. Burns a shifter's nose something awful." I said, before dropping my finished cigarette on the ground and putting it out with my boot.

Elex inclined his head as I called my wings launching myself into the sky. There was no point in being on a date with Archer if our relationship was going to be focused on duties.

The skies were clear as I flew over Mercy Valley, forcing me to pull on the magic I usually saved for my beast form, to make myself invisible. I headed into the mountains, landing in a private spot to call on my beast, "Are you in the mood to fly?"

"Always." She responded, and I felt the change begin to roll over

my body. The shift was completely seamless, the magic in my bones stretching and molding until I was in my Dragon form. Stretching my wings toward the sky, I let out a roar that had been itching in my throat for days. The ground shook from the force of it, but I didn't care. I launched myself back into the sky, my invisibility keeping me hidden from human eyes. My beast was in full control as she released a stream of blue fire from her throat. I slid to the back of my mind, relishing in the peace of my beast form. I'd been neglecting myself for months, trying desperately to find my mates and fulfill my role as Queen. On top of the hunt for my mother's killer it was all becoming too much. I was only a twenty-one-year-old girl. I should have been in college, getting drunk with my friends, and having sloppy sex with random frat boys. Instead, I was expected to rule over twenty Dragon Clans. Crying was different in Dragon form. The noise of despair that left my throat was a high keen. It reverberated in the air around me, as if even the wind felt my pain and sought to escape it. Months of rage, fear, and sadness poured out of me. Helplessness and hopelessness had grown in me until finally I had nothing left. My mother was gone, my dads could pass at any time, my mates were disappointing. It was too much for me to even begin to process. I wanted nothing more than to disappear into my beast, running deeper into the mountains until I was feral and none of my duties mattered. I just couldn't...

I skimmed along the clouds, lost in the freedom of my beast. She had pushed me deep into our shared mind, allowing me time to grieve and process. I loved her. While my dragon was a part of me, we were separate consciouses that coexisted in the same body. We shared our lives more intimately than mates. I had never appreciated her more than I did right now. I closed my eyes, letting myself fall asleep, leaving my beast alone.

I AWOKE to the sound of a rumbling roar vibrating my bones. My beast nudged me, *"You're going to have to deal with this."*

"What did you do?" I asked, groggily.

She didn't answer my question as she landed near our home. I was once again in the pilot's seat of my mind, but I was staring into the red eyes of a giant green dragon. It took me no time to realize that this was Archer's beast. I shook, forcing my body to shift back into my human form. I kept my wings out just in case I needed to get away quickly. I was far faster by wing than my human legs.

Archer didn't change immediately, his massive form towering over me. The shirt I wore was nearly the same color as his scales. I wondered if my beast had known that when I'd selected it this morning. Dragons perceived more than their human counterparts could.

"We can't communicate like this." I pointed out, not breaking eye contact with Archer's beast. He huffed, but slowly began to shrink and change.

"You made me hunt you down." He growled, "You left our date and then made me chase you all the way out here."

I held in a snort. He'd earned that with his shitty speeches, "You didn't have to chase me." I responded. Of course, that was bullshit. Dragons were predators, we couldn't resist the chase. Especially if it was our mate.

"You're a brat." He growled again, stepping closer to me, "This behavior should be punished."

"You put a single finger on me without my explicit consent, and I will send my deepest condolences to your mother. Hard to reproduce for her with no cock." I snapped back. "How about you just stay the fuck away from me until your mother arrives for our mating ceremony. We will do our duty to our people, but I see no reason to endure each other's company otherwise."

Archer took a step back like I'd slapped him. He cleared his throat, "If that is what you wish. We will need to make a few public appearances for my entourage and your fathers."

I nodded, "Of course."

"Alright then... See you around, Princess." Archer launched himself into the sky without another word.

I took a deep breath, letting the shaking in my hands spread across my body the way it had been desperate to the entire time I'd been talking to him. Pain renewed itself in my chest. My fate was sealed. One mate who wanted to remain a servant and another who would only be a mate in reproduction. Maybe that was all that I deserved after being the reason my mother was out when she was shot.

A FEW DAYS passed in a whirlwind of meetings, fitful sleep, and a deepening depression I could barely sit up through. I wanted nothing more than to curl up in my bed and hide there until all of the people milling around our home left. I had no will to live, dark bags had taken root underneath my eyes, and this morning I'd noticed my pants were loose. A dark part of me wanted to join my mother in death. Instead, I was subjected to another lunch with my father's insistence on my cooperation.

"Are you even paying attention?" Papa asked, exasperated.

"Fallon, it's important. We almost have a deal with Lord Hambridge. We're going to need you to sign off on it. Hambridge wants you at the final meeting tomorrow." Dad explained.

"Does it release Bain from any form of servitude to the Hambridge Clan?" I asked, finally interested in what they were saying.

Dad nodded, but the lines on his face told me there was more, "Yes, Bain will be free to rule as King and be your mate. Lord Hambridge just... He's demanding that we provide him with a servant in return."

"What?" I shouted, standing from my seat, "You've told him no, I assume?"

Papa and Dad glanced at one another, "Mateo has offered-"

"Absolutely fucking not. Mateo is part of this family. He is not leaving to serve Lord Hambridge." I said, slamming my hand down on the table. "I will turn every member of Clan Hambridge to ash before that happens. Do I make myself clear?"

Strangely, Papa grinned, "You sound like your mother."

"We have a plan, but we need your cooperation, Fallon. Lord Hambridge needs to feel like he won something." Dad said.

"He's won if he leaves here with his life." I grumbled, "I'll do whatever you ask me to."

"Thank you. Now tell me, how are things going with Archer?" Papa asked.

I hoped my cringe didn't show on my face, "Fine."

"Just fine? You're in the early stages of your mate bond. Fine is not how you should be describing it." He said, eyebrows furrowed.

"What's going on, hatchling?" Dad asked.

I wanted to tell them the truth about Archer, but it would only bring them pain. So instead, I said, "We're taking things slow. I'm sure we'll be ready for our mating ceremony when Queen Phaedra arrives."

"If you're sure..." Papa said, before he changed the subject. "We got responses from all the Clans that had sent people except the Faelor Clan of Scotland. They haven't responded to our calls or letters."

"Thank god. I am tired of hosting." I said, glad of the subject change, "I'm sure Clan Faelor is just busy."

"Once you've sealed your bonds with your mates, you'll be able to focus on taking on your duties as Queen. Not much longer now, Fallon." Dad said, trying to comfort me. Instead, a sense of dread filled me, but I couldn't let them know how terrified I was. It wasn't their job to fix the problems in my life. They had done enough for me. Soon they'd pass on to be rejoined with Mom. I wanted them to go in peace. So instead of responding, I nodded and smiled. I could pretend to be happy about sealing the bonds.

"Why don't you go relax, Fal. It's been a very busy few days." Papa offered, reading my emotions better than I would have liked.

"If either of you need me, I'll be in my rooms." I said before I left their office. I took the stairs to my room two at a time, praying that I wouldn't run into Archer or Hambridge on my way. Once I slipped inside, closing and locking my door I let loose a sigh of frustration. I stomped my foot down to hold in the scream that was building in my chest.

"That was the most childish thing I've ever seen." I jumped at the monotone voice that floated through my window. I whirled around, my beast pushing to the front to find the threat. Of course, Willow Ashcroft couldn't truly be considered a threat. I took her in, the black hair that reached just past her jawline, deep green eyes, and skin so pale you could nearly see through it. I hadn't seen her in nearly four years, but only the deep purple marks under her eyes had changed. She looked about as bad as I felt.

"Well, I assumed I was in the privacy of my own room." I responded, "Glad you finally decided to show up."

"It's a long drive from Oregon to Tennessee." She shrugged, before dropping onto my bed, "Now, what was your favor, Fallon Eyre. I don't want to be here any longer than absolutely necessary."

"My mother was killed almost six months ago. Three gun shots, close range to the back of her skull. The bullets were silver to be sure it would kill her. I've been hunting her killer, but my freedom to do so has come to an end. I want you to do your freaky little communing and tell me what the dead know." I rushed through the explanation, forcing myself not to show a single emotion on my face.

Willow was silent for a long moment, before she sighed, "Do you have any leads? I don't want to just seek out information aimlessly."

"Cecil Vaegra was spotted near where she was found, about ten minutes before she was killed." I said.

"That's not much." She grumbled, "You're lucky I owe you for getting me out of town." When I was eighteen and Willow was twenty-one, we'd met at a bonfire party some shifters had thrown. That night was still somewhat fuzzy in my mind, but it had ended with the Ashcroft family home burnt to the ground due to some freaky ghost shit. When Willow had run from her family with nowhere to go, I'd used my mother's connections to get her out of town with enough money to start a new life somewhere else. I liked Willow, but her secrets ran deeper than my own. Which meant I could never trust her.

"How long will it take for you to find information?" I asked, itching to know how close I was to finding my mother's killer.

"I need to know one thing…" She trailed off, meeting my eyes, "Do you want me to contact your mother?"

I stopped breathing, my racing heartbeat filling my ears. I desperately wanted to talk to my mother, but I couldn't face her. Not after she had died because I'd been a stupid drunk teenager, "No. Not unless it's absolutely necessary."

She stared at me, causing me to shift uncomfortably. Willow was perceptive, reading me better than anyone I'd ever met, "Okay. Give me a couple weeks. I'll come back when I have information."

She stood to leave, but I stopped her with a hand on her shoulder. She flinched at the touch, but didn't shake me away, "Thank you for coming… I don't trust anyone else with helping me find her killer."

She gave me a sharp nod before stepping onto the balcony. I blinked and she had disappeared as if she was one of the ghosts that she so often communed with. Willow was the strangest person I'd ever met, which was a crazy thing to think considering I often rubbed elbows with all sorts of different creatures' humans believed to be myths.

I stripped out of my clothes and climbed into my bed, exhausted even though I'd barely done anything all day. I could do nothing but wait. Wait to be mated to men who didn't want me. Wait to find out who killed my mother. Wait for my fathers to die. As my mind spun, tears began to leak down my cheeks. I did nothing to stop them. Feeling my despair was the only thing I could do right now. So, I basked in it, letting sorrow pull me into darkness.

I OPENED my eyes to complete darkness. A strange sense of being watched filled me. At first my tired mind couldn't figure out what had woken me, but my beast pushed forward, speaking in my mind, "*Mate.*" That's when Bain's pine scent finally reached my nose. I sat up, my eyes zeroing in on the hulking form that stood at the corner of my room.

"Hello Bain." I said, holding the silk topsheet of my bed over my naked breasts I stood.

"Hello Princess." His voice was low, so low I barely heard it.

"Why are you here?" I asked.

"I can't stay away." He whispered, "You need to tell your fathers to send me back with Lord Hambridge."

"I will not." My voice raised above the quiet tones we'd been speaking in, causing Bain to flinch. I softened, "You are my mate, a future King of the Dragons of the Occydent." He just shook his head. Without a second thought, I dropped the sheet from my body, stepping into the moonlight that streamed through the balcony doors. Bain's sharp inhale was the only warning I got before he grabbed me. I gasped as his lips crashed down on mine, his hands roaming over my naked sides. I moaned as his tongue swept between my lips, melting into his embrace. When I moved to wrap my arms around his neck, he pulled away. His eyes were wild, glowing with the power of his beast. He panted for a moment, before taking a couple of large steps and disappearing out the balcony doors.

I growled, my beast and I both frustrated with our mate leaving us. I glanced to my rumpled bed, unsure that I'd be able to go back to sleep after our encounter. After pacing for a few moments, I slipped into my bathroom. The porcelain clawfoot tub sat underneath a stained-glass window that depicted a dragon in flight. The dragon was actually my mother; her golden scales glistened in the bright moonlight. I turned the water on letting it fill the tub until steam billowed across the room. As I climbed in, I stared up at the depiction of my mother, "You know if you hadn't died, I would probably be out partying right now. You would be awake, just waiting to tell me off for forgetting my duties as Princess..." I trailed off as a tear rolled down my cheek, "I miss you, Mama. I don't know if I can be half the Queen that you were."

The room was silent as my tears mixed with the warm water of my bath. I stayed there until the sun began to rise, illuminating the window I'd been staring at for hours. I sighed, exhaustion finally rushing through my bones. I would sleep until it was time to meet with Hambridge. Maybe my dreams would grant me some new sense of how to handle my strange mate.

Pounding on my door brought me awake. I rushed to open it, glad that I'd dressed myself in simple green leggings and a black tank top before I'd passed out.

"Princess, you have a guest to greet in the hall. Now." Mateo said.

"A guest?" I asked as I followed him down the stairs.

"Apparently, Clan Faelor didn't get the message that you had already found the next kings. They had sent their only eligible dragon. He flew here, so there was no way for him to be contacted." He explained as we rushed toward the throne room.

The moment we entered, my eyes fell on the huge man in the center. His soft, curly brown hair spilled across his forehead. His biceps were easily triple the size of mine, and his broad chest led into a cute, round tummy. The simple white shirt he wore barely contained the sheer size of him. When his warm brown eyes met mine, we both froze. The scent of cinnamon and sugar met my nose, causing my eyes to widen. Before I could react, the man was before me, wrapping me in the tightest hug I'd ever been given, "'Ello, mate." His accent would have given away where he was from if I hadn't already known. Everyone in the room was silent as we embraced. Warmth flooded through my body, a sense of happiness overwhelming me as this giant man rubbed his cheek against mine. "Such a beauty." He rumbled.

A throat clearing caused us to pull apart, but my new mate didn't go far, staying within my reach as we turned to see my Dad staring at us. "What is going on here?"

My mate grinned, "Ma name is Marlow Faelor, son o' Tormund Faelor of Clan Faelor. I did not receive yer message about the Princess's mates. Seems that was a good thing, as I have now found my mate."

Dad's eyes widened, glancing at me, "Fallon, is this true?"

I nodded, too dumbstruck to speak. A third mate was... unexpected. There hadn't been a Dragon Queen in eleven centuries with more than two mates. "Marlow, your mate is Princess Fallon Eyre. It seems the Dragons of the Occydent have been blessed with three Kings."

The room erupted into chaos as everyone who had been silent began to speak at once. I simply tuned them out, turning toward the back exit in a haze. Three mates. I had three mates. I would be the first Dragon Queen in centuries to have more than two mates. As if my life wasn't complicated enough. A warm hand gently gripped my shoulder before I could reach the stairs. "Ye should never run from yer mate, Princess." Marlow voice was like a warm hug as he turned my body to face him.

"Sorry." Was the only word I could find as I searched his face. It was clear he was older than me. I knew Archer was only two years my senior. With Bain it was unclear, but Marlow showed his age visually. "How old are you?" I finally asked, breaking the silence.

He chuckled, "I'm thirty-four... You are in distress. What do you need? Our mating will be at your pace. No need to feel pressured to rush. I'm sure your other mates will-" A half laugh, half sob left my throat as soon as he mentioned my other mates. Once the sobs had started, I was unable to stop. Marlow wrapped me in his tight embrace, hoisting me off the ground. I didn't pay any attention as he carried me off. When he sat me down on my own bed I was surprised, but he explained, "I followed yer scent. Now, tell me what is wrong."

I didn't know where to start, but my beast pushed forward, "*Tell our mate everything.*"

I sighed, but then I began to spill days of pent-up emotion, "My mother is dead, my fathers are dying. My first mate is a lying piece of trash Prince who only cares about duty. My second mate is a literal slave. I swear every day my life just spirals further out of my control." By the end I was sobbing again, my words slurred and rushed. Embarrassment flooded me as I realized I'd completely broken down on this man. Mate or not, it was weak.

Marlow wrapped me into his arms, picking me up and sitting back on the bed until I was cuddled in his lap. "Yer a strong woman to handle all of that and still function... But I want you to stop trying to control everything. Life is never going to stop throwing us curve balls." Marlow said once I had calmed down enough, "Worry not my pretty mate, I will stand by yer side no matter what. Yer other mates may not be there for ye now, but the draw to a mate is impossible to ignore. They just need time... But if they don't get their shit together, I'd be happy to have ye to myself."

I snorted, "Thank you, Marlow."

"Do not thank me for basic kindness, Fallon. It is my job to spoil, love, and be by yer side until the end of our days." He said, pressing a soft kiss to the top of my head.

We sat that way for a long time, until suddenly my bedroom door swung open. My fathers stormed in, fear and rage painted across their faces. They stopped when they took in the scene. No one moved or spoke for a long moment, finally Dad said, "Fallon, we have a meeting with Lord Hambridge in five minutes."

I slapped my forehead, "Fuck. I forgot. Give me just a minute."

"We need to discuss your... situation afterward." Papa said, looking over Marlow suspiciously.

"What is there to discuss? The Princess has been blessed with three mates." Marlow responded, and I felt the tension in his muscles as I began to climb out of his lap.

My fathers shared a meaningful look, but neither responded. Instead, I stood, stretching my limbs before I said, "Lead the way."

We walked in silence to the small meeting room located closest to my rooms. Lord Hambridge was already sitting in one of the plush wing backed chairs. Bain stood off to his right, eyes downcast, discomfort and sadness radiating from him. "You certainly took your sweet time." Hambridge said in lieu of greeting.

I tensed, but forced myself not to react. My beast slumbered in the back of my mind, unwilling to deal with the farce that was this conversation. I saw no point in trying to deal with a man who was known for keeping servants, but my fathers were more well versed in politics than I was. I trusted their judgement far more than my own right now.

"Thank you for your patience, Lord Hambridge. The Princess has found an unexpected third mate. We were delayed celebrating this unexpected boon." Papa said.

Lord Hambridge's eyes widened, but he said, "Well, let's finalized our deal. Have you already explained the price of her mate to the Princess?" For the first time I finally saw Hambridge's true cruelty. He was a truly evil man who enjoyed the suffering of others. I wanted to snuff out the light in his eyes, but I forced my feet to stay rooted to their spot on the carpet.

"We wanted to discuss our terms further." Dad began. "We are willing to send you with a servant, but we will not agree to have him bound as you have bound your other servants."

"Why would I agree to that? Bringing an unbound servant into my home that is loyal to you... You really must think I'm stupid." Hambridge responded.

For the first time I saw my father begin to lose his cool. A growl rumbled through his chest, "You dare insult the crown further? The laws of our people aren't in your favor here, Hambridge. The only reason we stopped our daughter from killing you is that Bain's contract would pass on to your young heir."

Hambridge was damn near purple with rage by the time Dad was finished speaking. I held in a laugh as he stuttered, "Well I... How dare... You can't treat me this way."

I had had enough. "I can and I will. In just a few months, I will be your Queen. I wonder if the Hambridge Clan will be happy with you for having made an enemy of their new Queen."

"Not just their new Queen, but the Queen of the Oryent as well." Archer's voice caused goosebumps to erupt all over my body. I tensed, but I didn't allow myself to look back at him. Tried not to wonder how he'd known about this meeting. I glanced to Bain, surprised to find that his eyes were on me. For the first time I saw hope in their blue depths.

Lord Hambridge's reddish purple face turned white as he took in Archer. He cleared his throat, loosening the tie he wore, "I would never purposefully make an enemy of either Queen. I think the offer King Chaska has made it completely reasonable."

Dad smirked at me as he pulled a stack of papers from the bag hanging on his hips, "You'll sign here, here, and there. We must witness the unbinding ceremony to ensure that Bainbridge Abasom is free from any commitment with you."

I raised an eyebrow as I learned Bain's full name but didn't comment as Lord Hambridge signed the papers with a flourish. When he turned to Bain, I wasn't prepared for him to produce a knife, grabbing my mate's arm and slicing down a small tattoo on his inner arm. I growled, but before I could jump forward to intervene strong arms wrapped around my mid-section lifting me from the ground. I stilled as Archer's orchid and ginger scent reached my nose. He whispered in my ear, "It's the only way to free him. Control your beast." His commanding tone sent a shiver down my spine that had me cursing my beast. While my human side may not want anything to do with Archer Dabel, my Dragon wanted to rub herself along every inch of him until they were no question that he belonged to us.

Lord Hambridge rolled up his own sleeve, showing off at least ten tattoos. He found one on his inner wrist, before slicing through it. Bain dropped to his knees, howling as whatever magic held him to his master severed.

Lord Hambridge straightened, before turning back to us, "It is done. I will leave at first light. Let your butler know he'll be returning with me."

No one spoke as he made his way out of the room. Once he was gone, Archer released me. I rushed to Bain's side, wiping away the tears that had trickled from his eyes, "It's okay. You're free now."

He stared at me for a long moment, as if my words were impossible to comprehend. "You should not have traded someone else's life for mine." He finally said, glancing to my fathers, "I've seen the way you treat Mateo. He is family to you. Even without the bond he will have a horrible life under Lord Hambridge."

"Close the door, Prince." Papa ordered. Once Archer had done so he said, "Mateo is far more than a butler. He has been a spy for the Eyre family for a century. He is not going with Hambridge to serve, but to destroy the entire Hambridge Clan from the inside." My mouth dropped open in shock. I had trusted them, but some part of me had always been planning to stop Mateo from leaving. "He'll be back home before your matings are complete."

"The games of royals." Archer said, nodding as if this level of subterfuge was normal. "Hambridge was stupid to accept any deal."

"He was stupid to try to keep the future Queen from one of her mates. Agana had been trying to end these contracts for years before she died. Hambridge is the final hold out. It is good to know that one of my final acts as King will complete her legacy." Dad explained.

A knock on the door stopped us from speaking further, but when Marlow entered, I relaxed. "The butler told me to come here." He explained, before taking the seat next to me.

"The four of you are just a few months shy of being the rulers of all of the Dragons of the Occydent. Fallon has been prepared for this possibility since before she could walk. Archer understands the level of responsibility that comes with this role, even if he never expected to end up in it. We wanted to talk to the four of you now that there is nothing standing between you and your matings." Dad started, "We aren't stupid, even if our daughter might like to think that we are. There is some clear tension between you. Figure it out. You don't have long before we are gone, and an entire population of Dragons will be answering to you." My mouth went dry. I had hoped they hadn't noticed the issues between Archer and I. "Bain, I'm going to get you in touch with a therapist. She's a tiger shifter, and will be able to understand the complexities of your situation. Talk to her, work through your trauma. And don't forget that you are meant to lean on your mate." Bain tensed, but gave a sharp nod. "Fallon will be the first Dragon Queen in over eleven centuries to have three mates. This is going to draw lots of attention. Good and bad. The three of you need to be a united front to protect her."

"That is our job as 'er mates." Marlow responded, as he placed one of his large hands on my thigh.

"Yes it is. And as the oldest among you, I expect you to lead the other three through their issues. They are barely more than hatchlings." Papa said.

I should have been offended by the comment, but it was true. Archer, Bain, and I would be the youngest rulers in about six hundred years. Whether I liked it or not that would be a challenge all on its own.

"Fallon, your uncle made contact. He'll be returning this week for your matings." Dad said. I smiled. Uncle Adam was my mother's younger brother. He'd always been good to me, bringing me gifts and playing with me anytime he was in town. Immediately after Mom was killed, he spent weeks with us, trying to hold us all together. If Dragons weren't matriarchal, he would have taken the throne. In some ways I wished he could have. It would have allowed me freedom from the responsibilities of Queen, but it would dishonor my mother's legacy. No, I would become Queen, regardless of what it took from me.

"We want to be honest with you. We can both feel the call to rejoin our mate getting stronger. We don't have much more time with you. We're going to start meeting with each of you, teaching you what we can about our duties." Papa explained, "Your lives are about to change drastically. We are serious when we tell you to lean on one another. No one else can understand the pressures of ruling like you can."

We all nodded. I could also feel my power growing, my beast gaining more and more dominance each day. When my fathers did die, the last of their power would transfer to me, and I would become Queen. They were saying months, but if the changes to my power were any sign it would be weeks at best.

A week had passed since Bain had been released from Lord Hambridge's control, and Marlow had arrived. The house was a whirlwind of activity as my father's, Mateo, and Archer's people prepared for Queen Phaedra's arrival. I hadn't spent much time with my mates since our meeting. It wasn't so much that I was purpose-fully avoiding them. I looked at it as giving them time to bond. The future Kings needed to have a good working relationship if our people were to continue thriving under my rule. In reality, I knew I was avoiding my mates. I could blame Archer and his secrets, but that wasn't entirely true. Marlow had been nothing kind to me, Bain was damaged, but it was me that was creating the rift now. Out of fear or self-sabotage, probably both. I didn't feel like I deserved them. Not while my mother's killer still roamed free. I barely left my room, keeping myself cloistered inside.

I shuffled through the papers on my desk aimlessly, not truly reading the reports Papa had handed to me to look over. All from Clan leaders requesting various forms of aid or conflict resolution. A knock came at my door, and I sighed with relief. I was tired of pretending to work.

I smoothed the simple white dress I wore before opening the door. All three of my mates stood there. Marlow had a grin on his face, exuding happiness from his every pore. Bain stood to his left, seeming more relaxed than I'd ever seen him. He gave me a small smile as our eyes met, causing my heart to squeeze. His journey to healing might be long, but at least he had the freedom to do so now. Finally, I glanced at Archer only to find his intense red eyes assessing me. I couldn't deny my attraction to him as my scent grew stronger with arousal. A smirk played across his face, and I seriously considered slamming the door shut.

Marlow must have seen the look on my face, "Please, let us at least talk for a few minutes."

I sighed, but opened my door the rest of the way. The room wasn't as clean as it had been after Bain had worked his magic, but I wasn't embarrassed as they glanced around my bedroom. "The sitting area is through here."

"Will we be moving into the conjoined suites your fathers currently reside in once we complete our mating?" Archer asked.

I tensed, but Marlow once again saved the day, "I think it would be more respectful if we allowed Fallon to keep her rooms. We can all move to this floor once we've mated. Eventually, we can remodel."

Archer considered his words for a moment, "That's... acceptable. We can tailor the floor to our needs."

I flopped down in a chair, motioning for them to each take a seat. Archer cringed as he looked over my terrible posture, but I couldn't bring myself to care. He didn't even want us to have a true mating. Why should I care what he thought of me?

"We wanted to talk to ye about courting dates. I know your first one with Archer was... less than desirable. He has agreed that Bain and I need to begin the courting process if we are all to complete the bonds over the next couple of months. I thought ye and I could go out this evening."

I sat up, some excitement finally entering me, "Do you already have plans or is it up to me?"

"It's yer choice tonight, Princess." He grinned, "Ye can show me around Mercy Valley."

I smiled, genuine and wide, "I'd like that." I noticed that Archer was tense, but it only made me happier. I hoped he was jealous. He'd had his chance and ruined it.

"I was going to take you out tomorrow. I haven't made plans yet. I hope that's okay?" Bain said, a slight pink in his cheeks.

"We can play it by ear," I gave him a soft smile.

Before Bain could respond, Archer interjected. "I've made us reservations at The Raven Lounge for nine on Thursday."

My eyebrows went up in surprise. The Raven Lounge was a steakhouse and bar owned by the corvid shifters of Mercy Valley. It was popular and almost impossible to get into unless you had the right connections. I nodded, "I'll be there."

Archer inclined his head, "We have discussed your... needs quite thoroughly. If we are to be successful rulers we need a strong relationship."

It was the closest to an apology that I was going to get, so I responded. "The Dragons of the Occydent can thrive under us, but only if we can all operate as one unit."

We all fell into silence. None of us was certain on how to truly move forward, a sense of awkwardness began to fill the room. I hated it. Mates should feel at ease around each other. Instead, none of us had any idea where to go from here. I knew it was my job to lead us, but I couldn't.

"Well why don't the two of ye get out of here. Fallon and I have a date." Marlow said, clapping his hands together.

Archer and Bain both stood. Bain leaned down, pressing a soft kiss to the top of my head. I was surprised, but my body warmed at the attention. He left the room without another word. Archer stared after him for a moment, before his intense gaze turned back to me. He gave a small bow, "I'll see you on Thursday, Princess."

I inclined my head respectfully before he finally left the room.

Marlow moved to my side instantly, "So do ye need time to get ready?"

"Nope," I said, popping up from the chair, "I know exactly where we're going."

MARLOW SEEMED nervous as I dragged him toward the small building, "Are ye sure this is what you want to do?"

I hesitated, "We don't have to if you don't want to."

"It just seems... unlike a Princess."

I deflated, "Oh... We can do something else."

I dropped his hand, turning back toward my car. Before I could take a step, Marlow grabbed me, turning me back toward him gently, "I'm sorry, Fallon. I did na mean that in a negative way. I am just... surprised."

"You think its childish." I said, ignoring the tears that pricked the back of my eyes.

Marlow shook his head emphatically, "Nay, I just... I'm just stupid." I snorted, and he smiled at me, "Take me inside."

I pulled him inside, squinting as my eyes had to adjust to the darkness. I couldn't help the smile on my face as I glanced around the laser tag arena. We were above it, where just a few parents milled about. I probably should have felt some kind of shame, since I was an adult, but I didn't. My parents had brought me here for the first time, on my eighth birthday. I'd been obsessed ever since.

"Two for 60 minutes." I said to the clerk as we approached.

"Good to see you again, Fallon. It's been a while." Paul responded. He was a human nearing his seventies. Paul had owned Laser Quest my entire life. I was glad to see him still running it.

"Adulthood has been kicking my ass." I sighed as he handed me two adult sized vests and our guns.

"Who is this big fella?" He asked, squinting.

"This is Marlow. He's my... boyfriend." I internally cringed at the description, but the humans of Mercy Valley were used to the eccentric ways of many of the locals. He wouldn't be too shocked if I showed up with Archer or Bain.

"You be good to my girl, boy." Paul said.

Marlow gave me a nod before we took the stairs down into the arena. Marlow barely fit into the extra-large vest he'd been given, but I managed to clip it around his massive chest. When I moved to put my vest on, he stopped me. He rested it over my shoulders, before running his hands down my ribs and clipping it into place. Goosebumps raised across my body at his touch, my breath hitching. My scent grew stronger, its sweetness filling the space. A growl rumbled through his chest, which only increased my arousal.

"Let's play, before I have to take you in the back room of a dingy game room." He growled out.

I inhaled, nodding as I handed him his gun. I was overcome by him. Marlow's very presence was enough to make my core throb. Something about him was so safe, yet I wanted nothing more than to see how he'd take me. My mates were all gorgeous and complex, but Marlow was different. Kinder, less brisk than most dragons. I wanted to know what had made him gentle.

Instead, I took a deep breath, following after him into the laser tag arena. I knew the place almost as well as I knew my own home. It didn't take long for me to find my favorite hiding place. Strategically set on the very top of one of the small towers that were scattered throughout the room. Humans wouldn't have the balance to get up here, but I could easily stay put, watching and shooting anyone who came near me. Marlow had disappeared, no matter how much I scanned for him, I never caught a glimpse of him. When everyone but Marlow and I had been shot I climbed down. Creeping slowly across the arena, I hunted for any sign of Marlow. His scent had invaded the entire arena, so it was impossible to pinpoint where he was.

When strong fingers suddenly closed around the back of my neck, pulling me against a hot, hard body I forced myself to stay silent. Marlow's scent was overwhelmed with lust, and I understood why when he finally spoke, "I can't control meself any longer, Princess. You are my mate, aroused and ready for me." He panted, the strain of holding back from claiming me clearly taking its toll, "If ye don't want this, you better say so now."

"I want you, Marlow Faelor. I've wanted you since the first moment I laid eyes on you. My perfect mate," I panted back. I was desperate, my panties soaked. I hadn't considered when I'd selected laser tag, that it would set off our dragon's prey instincts. Or maybe I'd known this would happen, and its what I truly wanted. To feel something other than pain for a moment. Either way it didn't matter, I was going to fuck my mate right now.

"Walk slowly toward the bathroom. Do not run, or I'll have to chase ye." He growled, "This isn't how I wanted our first time together, but it is what my beast demands."

"I don't care what our first time is like, because it won't be the last." I said, leaning up to kiss his cheek, "Now come get me." I sprinted away, laughing as his growl echoed around the arena.

My steps pounded in my ears, as I rushed toward the single stall bathroom in the far corner of the arena. I could hear Marlow's huge body rushing after me, but it didn't stop me from skidding into the door. I pushed it open, but before I could step inside I was ripped off my feet and pressed against a cool concrete wall. "I knew ye were going to be a brat when I first laid eyes on ye." Marlow growled, "But that's okay, because that just gives me a chance to punish you with my cock."

My vest was ripped off, followed quickly by my dress and panties. I groaned as Marlow pressed thick fingers into my dripping pussy. "Already so ready for me, pet? The chase turns you on doesn't it? Soon we'll let our beasts play in the woods."

"Please, Mar, please just take me." I begged as he pumped his fingers slowly, curling against my g-spot.

"Your begging is so pretty, but I have to punish you for running." He said, before licking over my sensitive neck, nipping my ears as he continued to finger me. Just as I was about to cum, he pulled away causing me to whine sharply. He laughed, and I heard the rustle of clothing. "I never imagined I'd take my mate for the first time in a public restroom, but somehow it couldn't be more perfect." The head of his cock teased my entrance, and I pushed back desperate for him to be inside me, but he gripped my hips, "Nay, pet. This happens my way. I choose how and when you receive me, is that understood?"

"Yes sir." I groaned as I rested my cheek against the cool wall. My nipples brushed it, causing spasms to run over my body.

"Ah such a good pet," He groaned, as he slowly pressed inside of me. His cock was huge, wider than any I'd ever encountered before. I spread my legs wider, ensuring he could fill every inch of me. As soon as he brushed against my cervix, my entire body spasmed with an orgasm. I was boneless as he fucked me raw and rough, snapping his powerful hips into mine relentlessly. When he reached around, and rubbed over my pulsing clit I was forced into a second orgasm. "I'm close, Fallon. Do ye want to bond?"

"Please Marlow, please." I cried, meeting him stroke for stroke. He grabbed my tits, playing with my nipples as he finished filling me. With our bodies connected, golden light flashed behind my eyes, our bond snapping into place. For the first time in months, I didn't feel completely alone.

"Hello pet." Marlow whispered into my mind.

"Hello sir." I whispered back.

And just like that, life was a little bit brighter. Marlow Faelor had entered my life unexpectedly, but he was exactly what I needed. I wondered what it would be like with Bain or Archer, but I shook those thoughts from my mind. Marlow was the only thing that mattered right now.

Quiet taps on my balcony window awoke me from the first truly restful sleep I'd had in months. When I found Willow standing there looking pissed, I was glad I'd insisted that Marlow stay in his own room tonight. I wasn't ready to share my space with my mates yet. Even if the thrumming bond in the back of my mind was a comfort.

"You sleep like the dead," Willow said as I let her in.

"You'd know." I shot back, "What have you found out?"

"Nothing you're going to be happy about." She grimaced, "None of the spirits around here saw anything the night she was killed. So much nothing in fact that I did a little looking, someone wove a spell to hide themselves. Whoever killed your mother had been planning it for a long time."

A chill ran down my spine at her words, but somehow that didn't shock me as much as it should have. "What's next?"

"You could talk to her spirit directly." Willow offered.

I shook my head, "Absolutely not. I'm not going to disturb her afterlife."

Willow shrugged, "I'll reach out to some of my contacts in LA, see if they have any ideas about the spell remnants I found. It'll probably take a couple of weeks."

"Just call me next time," I said, turning back toward my bed.

"Fallon, if you're avoiding something by not talking to your mom... It won't help as much as you think. Sometimes the only good part of my abilities is that they can give you closure." Willow said.

Before I could respond, she had disappeared from the balcony as if she'd never been there. I crawled back into bed, my mind racing with thoughts of my mother and her murderer. Who would have spent months planning her death and have the resources to use the type of spell Willow described? Witches were notoriously hard to work with. Why had no one else picked up on the use of magic? I knew my dads wouldn't have been looking for it, but I would think that one of the other investigators would have. In the morning, I would find out who all had worked her case. Maybe it was time I paid the Mercy Valley Police Department a visit.

It WAS EARLY the next morning as I slid into the supple leather seats of my emerald, green Mustang. I hadn't driven my car in weeks, but it was always better to take it when I was going to see a lot of humans. Just as I was about to pull out Bain's face appeared in my window.

"Good morning, Princess Fallon. I was... Our date was supposed to be today. Do you still want to do something with me?" His blue eyes still held a sadness that broke my heart.

"Are you okay with running an errand with me first?" I asked. He gave me a small smile, and nodded, "Get in."

We drove in silence for several minutes before he asked, "What are you going to do?"

I debated for a moment how much I should tell him, but finally I said, "You know my mom was murdered a few months ago?" He nodded, reaching out a large hand to rest on my shoulder in a comforting way. "Well, I've been trying to find her murderer ever since. Today, we're going down to the police department. I... found some evidence of a spell. I want to know why no one else has mentioned it."

"I'll help anyway I can." He responded, seriously, "Your first act of Queen will be vengeance."

The words racketed through me. "That was very sexy, Bain. Careful or my beast and I might jump you."

"I can only hope." He smirked.

I laughed, and we fell into another comfortable silence. Every chance I got I ran my eyes over his profile. The strong nose, slightly crooked from being broken at some point, the full lips, and strong jaw made him beautiful. The scarring across his face and arms gave him an imposing look, but they didn't detract from his looks at all. "Keep your eyes on the road, Fallon." He said.

"So sorry for admiring my mate." I winked, but I kept my eyes on the road as we entered town.

The mood in the car shifted as Bain took in the sights of Mercy Valley, a sense of sadness seemed to come over him. He sighed, "Fallon... I don't know how to properly court you. I never thought I would find a mate. Much less a Princess. You know far more about this world than I do."

"You don't need to know how to court, Bain. Just be yourself." I said, "That's all that really matters to me anyway. I just want to be with you."

He snorted, "Why? I'm fucked up. I've never been to a movie, I've never drank, I don't know how to drive. I'm probably going to be in therapy for the rest of my days, just to deal with how fucked up my life has been."

"That just means I get to introduce you to all the things you've missed out on. Don't let Hambridge steal our happiness after he stole your freedom for so long." I argued.

"My therapist told me I should talk about it..." Bain trailed off, a haunted look in his eyes. When he continued, his voice was monotone. Detached. "My mother died before I hatched, by the time I was old enough to understand anything, my father was deep in his bottles. At nine, Hambridge showed up. My father owed him thousands of dollars... He offered my servitude to keep his life." Bain laughed harshly, "He was dead months after he struck the deal, but that changed nothing for me. Hambridge handed me off to his most brutal soldiers for training. I stayed with them in the Pits for years. When I was fourteen, Hambridge pulled me out. At first, I was thankful, until I realized he was training me to be his glorified butler. His personal bodyguard and servant..." Rage pulsed through my body at the story, but I forced myself to stay calm as he continued. "I've been shackled my entire life, Fallon. I don't know how I could possibly be a King, much less your mate."

"I don't care about any of that." I said as I parked the car, finally turning to take him in fully, "All I want to do is love you and be loved in return. We'll figure out ruling, Archer and I have been trained since birth for that. Your experiences will give you an unique perspective. Maybe together we can outlaw servitude contracts in the Clans?"

His breath hitched, "That's an option?"

"My mother had already been making progress. Hambridge was one of the few hold outs in the Occydent." I explained, "We have hundreds of years together, Bain. I know he stole your childhood, but you have your entire life ahead of you."

"If it's by your side I can't imagine anything better." He breathed, leaning closer. I closed the gap between us, our lips meeting in a mix of desperation and understanding. He tasted of oranges and coffee. I groaned as his hand wrapped around the back of my neck, pulling me closer. Before we could go further, a small knock on my window pulled my attention away.

I rolled it down and grinned at the police chief, a wolf shifter named Conri Lowell. "Hey Chief, I was coming to see you."

"Well, you're parked illegally, Princess, and the windows were getting awfully foggy." Bain turned pink at his words, but I laughed, "Why don't you park around back and meet me in my office."

I saluted him, before moving my car where he'd directed. Several of the shifter officers greeted me as Bain and I made our way to the Chief's office. "How do they know you so well?"

"I grew up the Mayor's daughter. Plus, my mother wasn't just Queen of the Dragons, she helped all the packs in the area. Eventually, so will we. Though I don't think I'm going to run for Mayor." I explained.

"Who is Mayor now?" He asked.

"Radley Beaumont, he's the father of one of the next High Alphas of the wolves. My mother worked very closely with him, so it was expected." I answered before we entered the Chief's office.

"What can I do for you, Fallon?" Conri asked as soon as I closed the door.

"I want to see my mother's case file." I announced casually.

His eyebrows shot up, "I can't give that to you, but why?"

"Yes, you can. Per the Tennessee Public Records Act of 1957, I can request any records as long as I'm asking the correct department." I shot back. Bain caught my eyes, a raised eyebrow and impressed look on his face. I just smiled in return. I'd spent my entire life watching the politics of Mercy Valley. My mother had harped on understanding the human laws our town was bound by. It came in handy every once in a while.

"You're too much like your mother." Conri sighed, "Why do you want them, Fall? You won't find any closure in them."

"How do you know?" I asked, leaning forward. Maybe Conri would tell me something useful.

"We're still looking for her killer but... It won't bring her back." The pity in his eyes was a blow to my ego. I saw what he must see. A young girl, barely an adult, grieving the loss of her mother. Badly. Bain laid a hand on my thigh, squeezing tightly. When I looked into his eyes, he shook his head slightly. What he couldn't say with his words, he conveyed with the hardening in his eyes.

I shook my head, "I'm running my own investigation as Dragon Queen of the Occydent, Conri. I need the files to see what you've missed."

At the mention of my title, he sat up straight, "I don't know what you think we've missed, but I'll give you a copy of the file." He stood, grabbing a thick brown folder, "Just remember, Fallon. If you think you've found her killer, let the human laws handle it."

"Only if her killer isn't a dragon." I said darkly, letting just a bit of my beast to the surface. "If they are, all you'll ever find is a patch of scorched Earth where they last stood." Conri paled at my words and hurriedly left to room to make a copy.

I strolled from the police station with the file tucked under my arm and a spring in my step. Bain was a step behind me, but before I could slip into the car, one of his arms banded around my middle. He pulled me against his body, and kissed me so soundly my head started to spin. "Do not ever let anyone convince you that you are meant to be Queen. Do you hear me, Fallon? You were made for this."

"I was made for you." I breathed, blinking the stars from my eyes.

"I'm slowly beginning to believe you." Bain said as he opened my car door. I opened my mouth to chastise him, but he stopped me, "I know I'm not your servant, but I do know what chivalry is. One of the very few things anyone taught me that was worthwhile in the Pit."

I kissed his cheek, and slid into my car. Once he was safely tucked inside I asked, "What would you like to do now?"

"Does Mercy Valley have a bookstore?" Bain asked, sheepishly.

I grinned, "We sure do."

Bear and Bees Books was tucked further into the mountains than most tourists were willing to go, but the owner, an old bear shifter named Urbana had no trouble keeping her small store open. Shifters from every clan and pack rushed to her store. It was more than just an adorable bookstore; it was a central meeting spot for many of us. I knew several shifters who had met their mate within its walls. As Bain opened the shop's buttery yellow door, the smell transported me back to my childhood. My mother would bring me here to socialize with the other young shifters while she had meetings with the leaders of the various species. I'd always been outgoing and friendly with everyone. Mom had always praised that quality, saying it was important for my future as Queen. I didn't always realize in the moment that she was teaching me the skills I'd need to replace her, but she'd ensured I could thrive without her. My smile dropped, but as soon as I laid eyes on Urbana sitting at her usual spot behind the counter it returned.

Her deep mocha skin was just showing the first signs of age. When she saw me, the wrinkles by her eyes became more apparent as she grinned.

"My sweetie dragon! To do what do I owe this honor, you haven't paid me a visit in months." She made her way around the counter, her bergamot scent wrapping around me as she enveloped me in what could only be considered a bear hug. "How are you doing?" She whispered, squeezing my biceps gently as she took me in. "Losing your Mama was one of the hardest things this community has been through since the Coyotes moved here."

"I'm... making it." I said, but I quickly changed the subject, "Please, let me introduce you to my mate, Bain."

Urbana was on him in a flash, running a thin hand over his muscular forearm, "Now aren't you a pretty specimen. Hotter than fire." I snorted, as she continued, "You had better be good to my lil sweetie dragon. She's an awfully special girl."

"I would lay down my life for her." He responded seriously.

"Good. Good." She patted him before turning back to me, "Are you looking for anything in particular?"

Before I could respond, Bain rubbed his arm. "Do you have anything that would help someone learn how to read and write better?" I had to stop my jaw from falling open. Did Bain not know how to read? I thought he'd wanted to come here because he liked reading.

"Basics or something for a certain grade level?" Urbana asked. There was no judgement in her tone.

"I comprehend the basics, but I only have an education to around second grade. I've picked up a few things over the years, but a King needs to know how to read and write letters." He explained seriously. I could see the deep blush on his face, letting me know he was embarrassed, but he didn't let that stop him from asking for help. I was proud of him, and I could see the same appreciation in Urbana's eyes.

"I've got a few things. Let me show you." They disappeared deeper into the bookstore. I beelined to the romance section, running my fingers over the colorful spines. I picked up several, until finally finding one that caught my attention. The four beefcakes on the cover gave me hope that I wasn't the only woman in the world that wanted multiple men to take me all at once. My mother may have had two mates, but there was always a clear distinction between when she spent time with Dad and when she spent time with Papa. I wanted to have Marlow, Archer, and Bain all at the same time as often as possible. Even though just the thought of Archer still set me on edge. I knew I'd have to face him tomorrow for our date.

Bain came back to my side; four books tucked under his arms. "Urbana offered to help me if I come in on Wednesdays when she's closed to stock the store." He spoke quietly, "Do you think that's okay?"

I smiled brightly, "Yes, I think that's a great idea."

He returned my smile, taking the book from my hands with a raised eyebrow, "Is this what you like to read?"

"Yes, it's part of a genre called reverse harem or why choose romance. The main characters have multiple partners." I explained as we walked back to the check out line.

"I can see why you'd enjoy reading that. Maybe you can read one to me soon." He suggested.

"They get a little... spicy." I said, unsure if he'd want me to read sex scenes aloud to him.

"Spicy? It's not edible, is it?" He asked.

Urbana snorted, "That's a nice way to say she likes reading sex books. Smut. Porn even."

"Urbana!" I gasped.

"Don't look at me like that, Fallon Eyre. I'm nearly two hundred years old. I know all about sex." She said, before winking at Bain.

"Alright, we're leaving." I said, snatching the books from the counter with a wink.

"Love you, sweetie dragon!" Urbana called after her with a laugh.

"You're a menace Urbana Jones! But I love you too." I shouted back.

BAIN and I had a quiet lunch at Mama's Place, before heading back to the house. I could tell he wasn't ready for more than a simple date, and I didn't want to push him to mate before he was ready. As we pulled up, I noticed a blue sedan that I hadn't seen in several months. "My uncle is here." I explained as I turned the car off. "He can be a bit... protective if you don't want to go in with me."

"You are my mate, Fallon. No one can scare me away from you now." Bain said, before climbing out of the car and rushing to open my door.

"I'm glad. Thank you... for staying. For letting us fight for you." I said, reaching up to kiss his cheek.

"No, thank you. Without your determination I would still be a servant to Hambridge. You gave me my freedom." He responded, "Never forget that."

We walked into the house, hand in hand, but I was quickly swept off my feet into a bear hug, "There's my perfect niece." My uncle boomed, "I was starting to worry, Fal. Where have you been?"

Uncle Adam sat me back onto my feet, "Bain and I just got back from our first courting date." I explained, motioning to where Bain had melted into the wall behind us.

"You better be good to my niece." Adam growled, "She's very special to all of us."

Bain nodded, "I'd never do anything to harm her, sir. I'll protect her with my life."

"Good answer." He winked at me. "He's seems like a good one, but I'm nervous about this seventh Prince of Queen Phaedra, your fathers were telling me about. The Dragons of the Oryent can be ruthless."

"I can handle my mates." I waved him off. I didn't want anyone else to know just how nervous Archer Dabel made me. I couldn't trust him, but I had no choice but to mate with him. Hopefully, tomorrow we'd find some kind of common ground.

ARCHER WAS silent as we walked through the halls of my home together. He had knocked on my door at seven am sharp, requesting that I join him for breakfast. I'd grumbled as I'd gotten dressed, annoyed at being woken up so early. As soon as we entered the kitchen, the smells made my mouth water. I hadn't had a home-cooked meal since my father's had dismissed the staff. In fact, my beast had taken to hunting in the evenings over eating normal food. The deeper I spiraled into the depression, the harder it was for me to eat.

"Did you make all this?" I asked, looking over the spread of pancakes, fruit, and various meats that had been prepared.

"I cook to relax. I've gotten quite good over the years." He responded, "Feeding a mate is an important part of creating the bond. I wanted to show you that I am capable of meeting your needs."

I stared at him for a long moment. He was too uptight; I could see the lines of strain at the corners of his red eyes. "It looks delicious. Thank you." I sat down, motioning for him to join me. I reached for a plate, but he snatched it from my hand. I watched as he added some of everything to my plate, piling it high with everything he'd made. Once he set my plate down, he looked at me expectantly, "Aren't you going to eat?"

He looked confused. "You should eat first."

"I'd prefer if we ate together," I said. He nodded slowly before making himself a plate. Once he was done, he sat down across from me. When he didn't immediately start digging in, I picked up my fork, taking a small bite of the fluffiest pancake I'd ever seen. It nearly melted on my tongue, the sweet flavor bursting across my taste buds. I couldn't stop the moan that left my throat, "This is delicious."

I glanced up, seeing that Archer was gripping his fork hard enough to bend it. He coughed as he met my eyes, "Apologies."

"It's natural to be attracted to me. You don't have to pretend you aren't." I said, trying to hide the smirk I felt curling across my face.

"I was raised to ignore my baser urges," Archer said, before stuffing a forkful of food in his face, effectively ending the conversation.

We finished our meal in silence. My thoughts raced, trying to piece together an image of Archer Dabel that made sense. None of what I'd seen so far fit together. His meeting with Cecil, his lectures about duty. They painted a picture of a no nonsense, uninterested asshole. But he'd stepped in when we'd been fighting with Hambridge to save Bain. He'd cooked me a delicious meal, one that he was clearly nervous to share with me. I could see potential in him, but it felt like he didn't truly want me.

"Did you ever want a mate?" I blurted out.

Archer's face remained neutral, but I could see in his eyes the way his mind drifted off. "Unlike your mother, mine had many hatchlings, as you well know. It was never expected that I'd do anything more than run the businesses my father set aside for me. I've spent my life focused on that. Mates were for other people. People with more time."

"What will happen with your businesses now?" I asked, before adding, "And what type of businesses are they?"

"There's a variety. We've got a medical equipment company that my youngest sister is going to be taking over since it is based in China. I'm maintaining control of our American companies, which are mostly restaurants." He explained, "You're not really interested in this, you don't need to force conversation."

"I'm interested in learning about you." I shot back.

"Oh..." He trailed off, "I want to learn more about you as well, Fallon."

"Well, that's a good starting place I think." I stood, "Why don't we go for a flight today?"

Archer raised an eyebrow, "I actually had made plans. I thought we'd go purchase your dress for our mating ceremony before our dinner at the Raven Lounge."

I laughed, "Why not both?"

"I'll drive us into town, I'm sure I can have one of my assistants pick up my car." He conceded. I beamed, happy that it seemed Archer and I were going to have a good day. Maybe we could learn to compromise, to find more common ground.

Before I could stand a nudge at the back of my mind drew my attention, Marlow was pulling on our bond. *Is everything okay?* I asked.

Your uncle asked me to get you, but you aren't in your room. Fallon... it's your dads. Marlow whispered into my mind.

My eyes grew wide, causing Archer to stop in front of me, "What's wrong?"

"I..." I stood, rushing out of the room. I flew up the stairs, my feet barely touching the ground as my wings popped out. My beast rumbled in my mind, *"They have been without their mate for too long. I've been smelling the decay on them for weeks. They need to pass on, to rejoin our mother."* Tears leaked from my eyes as she spoke into my mind. It wasn't supposed to happen yet. They were supposed to be here when I took over as Queen, to be by my side during the mating ceremony for Archer and I.

I burst into their room, panting and panicked. My uncle sat in the corner of the room, while Dad and Papa laid side by side on the bed that had once belonged to my mother. I went to Papa's side first, brushing his grey hair from his forehead, "Papa, it's Fallon. I'm here."

"My flower." His voice was harsh, as if he hurt for him to speak, "Our time together draws to an end. I can feel your mother calling me to her."

Tears ran down my face unchecked, "It's okay, Papa. You can go to her."

He smiled, reaching up to touch my face, "I am so proud of you, Fallon. Everything wonderful about your mother lives on in you." When his hand dropped down to the bed, his breathing slowed. His chest barely moved.

I moved to Dad's side. He was more alert, "Do not shed tears for us, daughter. We are returning to your mother."

"I can't help it, Daddy." I cried, laying my head on his broad chest, "I'm going to miss you. I still need you and Papa."

He tangled his fingers into my hair, holding me to his chest for a long moment. I was transported back in time, to my childhood when he would hold me at night when I couldn't find sleep. His breath hitched, and I moved, looking into his face. "Fallon Agana Eyre, you are destined to be Queen of the Occydent Dragons. You will not falter, do you understand?" I nodded, not trusting myself to speak at first, "I know you are young. Younger than most of the Queens before you, but I have no doubt you will..." He stopped, coughing until he was out of breath. "You will do great things. Just remember to lean on your mates."

I backed away as he closed his eyes, sinking to my knees on the floor beside their bed. Warmth wrapped around me, and I found myself glancing into the deep red eyes of Archer. Without a word he had followed me here, and now as I watched the final moments of my fathers life slip away, he held me. An unwavering ship in the stormy sea of my grief. Tears ran down my face unchecked, my chest tight with pain. Through all of it Archer did not move. His arms banded around me like they could hold me together. Maybe they would.

I have no idea how long we stayed like that before a man I didn't recognize entered the room. "My sincerest apologies, Princess. Your Uncle has called me to pronounce their deaths."

I glanced to Adam, who had been silent since I entered the room. He gave a small nod, "Go, Fallon. Grieve. I can handle things until you're ready."

Archer didn't give me a choice; he lifted me from the floor with ease, carrying me from the room as sobs began to shake my entire body. It didn't matter that I'd known they would die; their deaths were another knife to my heart. Another reason not to go on, because everyone I loved died. I barely recognized when Archer sat me on my bed, disappearing from the room. I curled into a ball, unable to do anything but cry as my world fell apart.

I didn't hear when Archer returned, but I was suddenly picked up and carefully positioned in the center of my bed. Bain and Marlow sat on either side of me, while Archer had arranged me in his lap. No one spoke a word, but they were there, hands on my body, and pain in their eyes as I fell apart. That was more than I'd had when my mother was killed. My mates were still here, not flinching as sobs and screams left my body. Even through my grief, hope began to bloom in me. It wouldn't be fast, but I would heal from this, and my mates would support me through it. Even Archer, who was slowly showing me a softer side of himself.

THERE WAS no fanfare for my fathers funeral. It was a quiet and dreary affair on a rainy Sunday afternoon. It felt appropriate that the sky would weep with me. As soon as their ashes had scattered into the wind, I shifted into my beast form, disappearing into the clouds to mourn alone. While my mates had attended to my every need since Dad and Papa had died, I needed time alone with my beast to clear my head.

"We should focus on finding our mother's killer." My beast rumbled as we soared, rain pelting against our scales. *"Our role as Queen will be threatened until they are brought to justice. It will send a message to the Clans of our strength."*

"Queen Phaedra arrives in less than two weeks." I pointed out as I watched the ground from the back of my own mind, *"Deer on your six."*

We spread our wings, coasting slowly lower as fire built in our belly. Once we were close enough, we released a perfect stream of fire. Seconds later, delicious deer meat slid down our throat. My beast landed, stomping out a few wayward flames before stretching out. Images of Archer filled my mind as my beast seemed to drift toward the back of our mind. *"We did not get to court with our pretty mate."* She rumbled.

"I know... Do you truly believe we can trust him?" I asked. While we shared a mind and body, her instincts and mine were different. Our perspective of people and the world surrounding us weren't always the same.

"A mate bond is sacred to shifters; betraying a mate would be unimaginable." My beast responded, *"There is no need to hesitate with our mates. They were made for us."*

I drifted to the back of my mind, where my beast usually resided. I needed time to decide what to do next. Once Queen Phaedra arrived, I would have to seal my bond with Archer. Then only my bond with Bain remained before I would ascend to the throne. I needed to talk to someone who knew more, but with both of my fathers gone, and Mateo still spying on Hambridge, I had no one to turn to. The Clan had many elders, but they would look down on me if I asked them for advice. I was going to be their Queen. It was vital that they only saw my confidence and strength.

My beast raised her head as the sound of wings flapping met her sensitive ears. I watched wearily from the back of our minds as an orange dragon, slightly smaller than us, landed nearby. Uncle Adam shifted back to human form immediately, "Fallon, you've been gone all day. Your mates are about to drive me insane with their constant chattering."

I snorted, causing a bit of smoke to leave my beast's snout. I could not imagine Archer or Bain chattering, but Uncle Adam had always been dramatic. His brown eyes softened, "It's okay if you need to take time to grieve, Fallon. I can handle running things until you're ready. I'm sure Queen Phaedra would understand if you postponed her arrival." I shook my massive head, breaking branches on the trees around me. "You'll have to shift back if you want to talk."

"Why is he here bothering us?" My beast growled.

I sighed, *"Just let me shift back."* She grumbled but switched places with me. I shifted back, shaking my scales until they melted into my normal human skin. "Sorry. I'll head back. I need to speak with my mates anyway."

"Fallon, wait…" Adam wrapped his arms around me, "You don't need to be strong. I'm serious about taking the time that you need. I'm sure I can convince the Clans to answer to me until you're truly ready to become Queen."

I hugged him back, "That's good of you, Uncle, but it is my duty to our people to take my place." With those words, I flapped my wings taking to the skies and returning to my home.

MARLOW WAS by my side the moment I landed on my balcony, "Pet, ye shouldn't be out in the rain like this."

I couldn't help the smile that broke out across my face when Bain appeared beside him with a towel and soft, warm clothes. "Here. The bath is already waiting for you."

Archer was sitting in the corner, typing furiously on his cell phone. "After you're dressed we're going to purchase your dress for our mating ceremony." He informed me, absentmindedly, "I don't think you need to stay in these four walls any longer."

"You could at least ask." I pointed out. Marlow and Bain watched our conversation with a little too much interest. With Marlow and I already bonded, Bain and I having had a successful courting date, Archer was the only outlier.

He looked up from his phone now, "You love shopping. I've seen your bank account and your closet. I don't need to ask, when I know what it best for you."

How had he gotten access to my bank account? I shook my head, annoyance causing smoke to drift from my nose. It didn't matter, he was out of his mind if he thought he was going to talk to me like that.

"Oh fuck." Marlow muttered, before pressing a kiss to my

temple. "I'm sorry, pet. Bain and I are going to leave ye two alone now." They scurried from the room together, shooting Archer disapproving looks.

"Do you want to try that again?" I asked, a hand on my hip.

"You're dripping water on the rug. Go get ready so we can go shopping." He ordered, crossing the room to loom over me. His red eyes flashed with warning.

Something in me couldn't resist, "This is my room, I'll drip on the rugs if I want to."

I watched as the tension in his muscles seemed to build. Something was eating at my standoffish mate, but I didn't know what. I wasn't ready for Archer's hand to wrap around my throat, squeezing lightly. "When I tell you to do something, I expect you to do it without so much argument."

"I am not your slave." I growled back, unperturbed by his grip on me. The scent of my arousal was thick in the room, but when his orchid and ginger scent reached my nose I knew I wasn't the only one being affected.

"Why can't you just make this easy?" He growled, releasing me to pace, "I am your mate, Fallon!"

I wondered if this was the first time I'd heard him use my name, but I didn't have time to contemplate it before he was on me again. "You're driving me insane. Your scent permeates every inch of this house; I've smelled nothing but chocolate dipped roses for weeks."

"It's your own fault," I breathed. "You refuse to be honest, you refuse to even try to have a-" His lips crashed into mine, cutting off my sentence. He filled my senses, the smell and taste of him a heady drug. He moved me with ease, never breaking the devouring kiss. Before I could blink I was standing naked in the bathroom.

"You want the truth?" He whispered, pulling away, "The moment I laid eyes on you in Club Shift, you have haunted my every thought. I can barely maintain my composure around you, and that's all I have."

"Why were you there? Tell me so I can believe you actually want me." I wasn't above begging if it got me what I truly wanted.

Archer gave a harsh laugh, backing away from me, "Fuck. You're not ever going to let what you heard go, are you?"

"No, I'm not. It's my duty as the future Queen to protect my people and Mercy Valley. The Dragons of the Occydent will not be weakened by a King that will not protect them." I snapped at him.

He ran a hand over his face, "Get in the bath." When I didn't immediately do as he said, he added, "Please. I can't focus with you bare before me. You know I cannot take you until the bonding ceremony, you don't have to torture me further."

I climbed in the warm, bubbly water letting my body sink beneath until only my head was visible. "I told you the other day that I run several businesses for my family, do you remember." I nodded, ignoring the pain of remembering that morning. "Well... One of the businesses I was running involved... the blood trade. I was hoping to establish a relationship with Cecil in Club Shift. He was hesitant since your mother had put an end to his last supplier."

"You said was. Does that mean it's one of the businesses your siblings took over when we met?" I asked, trying not to react to the information he provided me.

He nodded, "What you overheard was just a shot at convincing him to work with me."

"Did he take you up on the offer?" I asked as I reached for a bottle of soap.

"He did not. Seemed too concerned with pissing you off." Archer responded, his red eyes tracking my every movement as I carefully washed myself. I couldn't help but rise out of the water slightly, letting him see the soap that covered my breasts.

"Maybe you should take a lesson from him." My voice was husky as I ran the washcloth lower down my body. My mate's eyes were glued to my every movement; I could see the way his muscles tensed. He was forcing himself not to react, but I wanted to see him come apart.

"You are a brat. I didn't believe Faelor when he told me, but you're certainly enjoying proving that now, aren't you?" I hummed instead of responding, sitting up on the edge of the tub and spreading my legs so he could see every inch of my bare pussy.

He let loose a primal sound before striding across the room and tangling his fingers into my wet hair. "I may not be able to fuck you yet, brat, but I can certainly punish you." He moved me so that I was bent over the edge of the tub, before I could prepare, he was raining down hard smacks on my wet ass. I moaned when one landed on my pussy, unable to stop myself from spreading my legs wider. "Such a naughty little thing to be enjoying your punishment."

"Archer please." I whined as he ran his fingers up and down my slit.

"Hmm, I can't wait to hear you scream my name next week." He said, before continuing his abuse of my bottom. When he finally stopped, tears ran down my face and my ass was hot. My core ached, desperate for my mate to take me. He helped me out of the tub, ensuring I was completely dry before handing me my clothes. "Now, you're going to be a good girl for me, right? I want to take you shopping for your mating dress today."

"This is certainly a very different attitude than, 'we must remember our duties.'" I mimicked with a snort. "What changed?"

"You." Was all he said before leaving me alone with a hot bottom and aching pussy. I cursed Archer Dabel as I slipped into the jeans and soft cashmere sweater that Bain had selected for me.

Em's Boutique was situated in the main square of Mercy Valley. During peak tourist season, it was nearly impossible to get inside the store. Thankfully, today, only a couple of people milled around. The owner grinned as I entered, greeting me with open arms, "Princess! It's good to see you." Emaline Potter looked to be in her mid-forties, but in reality, she was pushing a hundred years old. Her mate, Isabella, owned Izzy's Intimates next door. They were both cheetah shifters who were part of the cat shifters that made their home in Mercy Valley. I knew the cat shifters didn't operate with exactly the same in hierarchy as the dragon or wolves, but I couldn't explain what Em and Izzy's roles were within their pack... If it was even considered a pack. I shook my head. Shame washed over me because I didn't know vital information about the shifters that lived in my town. My mother had been protecting them for years, and I'd never even taken the time to understand their pack dynamics. "Hi Em. I'm here to buy a dress for my mating ceremony."

Her eyes widened, before landing on Archer who stood at my back silently taking in the space. "I didn't know you'd found your mates! The gossip clearly isn't making it way to my ears these days. Come on, come on, we have to find you something perfect!"

I laughed as she dragged me to the formal section. She hummed as she flipped through the racks, grabbing random dresses in varying colors and styles. She ushered me into a dressing room, "Naked girl, get naked. We have to find the perfect one."

I didn't hesitate, slipping from one dress to the other in a whirlwind. Nothing was right. Either the wrong color, yellow would forever wash me out, or too formal for the primal event I'd be participating in.

Em tsked as I handed her the final dress with a shake of my head, "I've got one last option, but it is... Well, I'll bring it to you."

She disappeared, leaving me naked and alone in the dressing room. I turned my back to the mirror, noticing a few faint bruises across my ass cheeks. Shifters' healing was accelerated, so I knew they'd be gone in another few hours, but the memory of Acher's punishment was enough to have me aching for him again. We weren't exactly where we should be as mates that were about to bond, but at least he'd given me some honesty today.

"Try this on." Em ordered as she stepped back into the room

without warning. The dress she'd handed me took no time to put on. I gasped as I looked in the mirror. The black silk hugged my body perfectly, accentuating what few curves I had. Cut outs along the sides and back gave teases of my skin without being scandalous.

"It's perfect!" I squealed.

"Finally," Archer said from outside the door, "I selected you some items from next door. I'll pay for the dress while you change."

"I can pay for it." I said, noticing the price tag was higher than anything else in my closet.

"No." Was all he said, before I heard the click of his shoes walking away. I wondered what he had bought from Izzy's, thrilled that my mate was showing an interest in me for the first time.

"He's a man of few words." Em said as I stepped back out of the changing room, "But he didn't even flinch at the price. You've got a fine mate there."

"It sure seems that way." I said, thoughtfully. Archer Dabel was far more than he had appeared on our first meeting, but I knew I had barely scratched the surface of who he truly was.

I PUSHED OPEN the door to my fathers study. I hadn't set foot in it since before they passed away, but I had tons of paperwork that needed to be done for the Clans. I'd received an email this morning from Radley Beaumont requesting an audience before my coronation. I'd typed up a quick response and shuffled out of my bedroom, knowing that the mountains of work could wait no longer. My uncle may have been helping, but it was my duty as Queen to care not only for the Dragons of the Occydent, but all the shifters of Mercy Valley.

I took a seat in the plush leather chair Papa had bought my mother last year for her birthday. I pushed away the tears that formed at the memory and started sorting through the papers on the desk. Anything urgent remained sitting in front of me, while everything else was filed into the appropriate box to be handled when I had more time. Once I bonded with Archer and Bain, my mates would begin to help me with these tasks. I needed to find out who would take over what duties. Marlow was certainly the friendliest. I planned to talk to him about handling relations within Mercy Valley. Archer clearly had a mind for business, so I'd put him in charge of our investments and any money or business issues the Clans faced. Bain had unique experiences that would make him an amazing advocate for the downtrodden. The future began to unfold in my mind, and for the first time in months, I wasn't terrified of what it might hold. My mates gave me hope for a future that had seemed all too bleak just a few weeks ago. I wasn't perfect. Too many mornings, I'd find myself lying in bed, paralyzed. My grief stuck in my throat, depression weighing down my every movement. But I pushed through. For my mates, my people, and ultimately for myself. My parents wouldn't have wanted my life to end because theirs did. I could feel the pain without letting it win.

"What are you doing in here?" Uncle Adam's voice broke the solemn silence of the office. "I told you to take your time to grieve. It's not a slow process."

I quirked an eyebrow at his tone, "I miss my parents, but they would not want me to lie around and ignore my duties as Queen."

"You aren't Queen yet. Why not wait until after your coronation?" He shot back.

I waved him off, "I'm only handling the urgent items. Don't worry about me, Uncle Adam."

He stared at me for a long moment before nodding. He turned to leave the room, but stopped at the door, "I don't think I realized just how much you've grown up, Fallon. I'm sure your mother would be very proud of you."

The words brought a small smile to my face. I could only hope that she was proud. I'd do anything to go back in time and change the night she died, but all I could do now was honor her memory. It would have to be enough.

BAIN KNOCKED on the study door, and I stood stretching my muscles, "Oh thank God. Are you here to save me from paperwork?"

His laugh was deep, and so full of joy I soaked in it for several moments. His transformation was well underway; he smiled more freely now and didn't flinch when one of us got too close to him. My mate was slowly healing from all he had endured. "I thought you might enjoy some lunch."

He nearly pushed me outside, and I spent several moments basking in the sun before he motioned for me to follow him. It was the first pretty day we'd had in several weeks, and I was glad to be outside enjoying it. We walked into the forest that surrounded us, and I raised a questioning brow at him. "Just trust me." He said, before entwining our fingers as we walked.

I gasped when he led us into a nearby clearing. There was a large red and white checkered blanket laid out on the ground, but the wicker picnic basket is what grabbed my attention. It was open, and overflowing with all sorts of bread, fruit, and cheese. I turned, throwing my arms around Bain, "This is so perfect."

He grinned, swelling with pride, "I don't know much about courting, so I did some research. A picnic seemed perfect for you."

"I love it." I beamed, before rushing toward the blanket to sit down, "Come join me."

He folded his much larger body awkwardly next to mine, and I instantly crawled into his lap. He seemed surprised at first, but wrapped his arms around my waist, pulling me in for a hug. We stayed like that for a long time, just embracing. His heat soaked into my body, warming not only my skin but something deeper. Bain's chest rumbled with something akin to a purr as I rubbed my nose over his cheek. "I can't wait for my scent to be entwined with yours the way Marlow's is." His grip moved lower onto my hips, causing my scent to grow stronger with my arousal, "So sweet and floral."

"We can bond whenever you're ready." I blurted out. When his eye widened I rushed to say, "Not that we have to now... Just whenever you want-"

"I want to bond with you too." He said, lust darkening his bright blue eyes.

I yanked the simple dress I'd been wearing over my head, revealing my nakedness. He didn't hesitate, his lips crashing down on mine. I felt his erection through his jeans, and reached down, palming him. I gulped slightly, shocked by the sheer size of him. I'd known he was broader than Marlow and Archer, but I didn't expect that to translate... everywhere. I wiggled away from his grasp, "Lay back, baby. I want to take care of you." I purred. He grunted but followed my instructions. I slowly undid his jeans, releasing his cock from its restraints. I licked the head, causing him to grab my hair pulling me away, "I... I've never done this before, Fallon. I don't want to disappoint you but-"

"You could never disappoint me." I said, before taking his throbbing cock into my mouth. He was too big to completely swallow, so I used one of my hands to slowly pump along the base of him. His muscles were shaking as I picked up the pace, swallowing him down until I gagged.

"Fuck, Fal, please... Bond..." He was panting, his eyes wild.

I felt powerful as I pulled away, before I slowly crawled up his chest, carefully straddling him. "I want to see you fall apart as I ride your cock." The stretch of his wide cock as I slowly worked my pussy down the length of him was painful, but my body was made for my mates. When he ran a thumb over my clit, my rhythm stuttered, but his other hand on my hip kept me moving. Bain's roar echoes through the tree as golden light flashed behind my eyes. Our bond snapped into place as my orgasm raced down my spine, soaking Bain's cock in my juices. I collapsed forward, lying on his chest as I spoke into his mind, *"You are finally mine."*

"I was yours the moment we met, I just didn't know how." He responded.

We laid together, basking in our newly formed bond. When Bain stroked the golden ring that sat on my pinky finger, I asked, "This must be special to you."

"It was my mother's. The only piece of her that my father didn't destroy in a drunken fit." He explained, "I never met her, but I like to believe that she would adore you."

I turned, kissing his cheek, "My mother would definitely have loved you. She would have taken you under her wing the moment she laid eyes on you."

"I'm sorry I never got to meet her." He pulled me to his chest, "I hate that we can bond over shared grief."

"Dead mom's club?" I joked halfheartedly. "Actually though... I appreciate it. Having someone who understand what it's like missing your parents. It helps."

We lapsed into a comfortable silence. The sounds of the mountains and Bain's heartbeat soothed me. We spent hours lying on the picnic blanket, enjoying the beautiful day and snacking on the food Bain had provided. I couldn't have planned a better bonding experience.

"That cloud looks like a turtle," I pointed out. My head was resting in his lap as we both stared up into the sky.

"Would you like to fly together?" He asked, "I can text Marlow to come clean this up for us."

"I'd love to." We carefully picked up our mess and left the blanket and basket out of the way nearby. Bain shifted first, giving me a fantastic look at the sheer size of his pure black Dragon. His beast was huge, probably twice the size of mine, with spikes running from the crown of his head to the tip of his tail. His beast nudged me with its snout, and I awoke my beast, allowing her to transform. I flapped my wings taking flight.

My beast soared through the skies, followed closely by Bain's beast. They communicated through body language and a series of roars that seemed to shake the sky around us. I rested in the back of our mind, basking in the glory of two of my bonded mates living within my soul. I didn't understand how my fathers had survived for so long without my mother. If something happened to Bain or Marlow, I'd want to die immediately. Sorrow filled my chest again; they had stayed far too long for me. Had sacrificed rejoining with their mate to ensure that I would be protected by my mates before I took the throne.

A loud noise drew my attention, but my beast's sudden roar ripped through my mind. Blazing pain flashed through my body.

"What happening?" I shouted.

"We've been shot." My beast growled, rage painting every corner of my mind, *"Left wing is shredded. I'm going down."* She panted to me. Her consciousness blinked out, and I was suddenly alone. The pain was blinding as I tried to flap my wing, desperate to slow our descent toward the ground.

A deep echoing roar accompanied the feeling of being jerked to a stop. I turned my head, finding Bain's beast, talons digging into my shoulders, carefully avoiding my wings. Fire smoked somewhere behind us, but I couldn't worry about that now. Pain was taking away my thoughts, turning me into a feral beast.

Bain's voice broke through the fog in my mind, *"Shift back, Fallon. Keep your wings."*

"I can't." I whined, *"I can't."*

"You will." He commanded, *"Just breathe through the pain, think of something else."*

"What? No. I can't." I was panicking as my vision blacked out.

"My therapist, Dani, she's part of the Pride in Mercy Valley. She's really helped me these last few weeks. I think you should go talk to her about your parents." Bain was rambling, but it was a perfect distraction. I reached for my beast, waking her. Together we slowly began our shift. I focused on my wings, forcing them to shrink, but remain out as my beast forced our large body back into human form. It wasn't a quick process, but Bain talked the entire time, *"She's taught me a lot, Fallon. I owe your Papa a debt of gratitude for forcing me to go. I'm making new progress everyday. I can see that you're still struggling, and there is no shame in that."*

Finally, I was back in human form. Bain landed a few feet from our home, shifting back to his human form just before Marlow and

Archer came running. "What the fuck?" Marlow shouted, "Who did this?"

"I don't know," Bain breathed hard, as Archer approached to inspect my injured wing, "We were just flying around. I heard the first shot, just assumed it was a hunter, but I saw the second bullet shred right through her wing."

"The good news is it did go through. We need to get the bleeding stopped. Her healing isn't kicking in." Archer said, "Take her to her room. Marlow, go find the bullet that pierced her. We need to know what kind it is. No regular bullet would cause this much damage to a Dragon's skin."

Marlow pressed a kiss to my head, before disappearing into the woods. "We've got ye, Princess. Just close your eyes."

The moment I closed my eyes; the pain and adrenaline caused me to black out.

"YE ARE na going out by yerself." Marlow's accent got thicker when he was angry. I couldn't imagine what he saw as I stood in front of him, arms crossed. My wings were still out three days later; the damaged one was partially wrapped in gauze. Whoever had shot me had used a silver bullet, ensuring that it would take me weeks to completely heal. My beast was still enraged about the attack, but we'd found nothing that gave us a single clue as to who could have shot me.

"I promised Radley Beaumont that I would meet him today at Mama's Place. I'm not cancelling over a little injury." I snapped.

Archer sighed from his place on the couch, "Someone tried to kill you, Fallon. How are you not treating this more seriously?"

I floundered for an answer to his question. Mostly because I hadn't let myself think about the reality of it too much. Whoever had killed my mother was still out there, and it looked like they were gunning for me now. It made no sense. I had assumed her death was due to a political rivalry, but I had nothing to do with the politics in Mercy Valley. "You guys can just come with me."

Bain, Archer, and Marlow seemed to have a silent conversation. I watched them, appreciating the bond that was clearly already forming between my mates. Finally, Archer sighed, "Fine. We all go, but I want you to know I am not happy about this."

"Your complaint has been acknowledged." I nodded, "Let's go."

Mama's Place was quiet as we entered, and Hannah, the hostess, nodded as I made my way toward the backroom. I had called ahead to warn them we were coming. As soon as I entered the room, I was struck by the smell of wolf. Radley wasn't alone; Conri and a beautiful woman I'd never seen before had joined him.

"Princess Fallon, I'm so glad to see that you're okay. Your Uncle reached out to me to let me know about the incident." Radley Beaumont stood to greet me. His eyes lingered on my visible wing. "We could have postponed until-"

"I'm fine, Radley. Introduce me to your mate." I'd smelled her scent on him as soon as he'd gotten close to me.

Her strawberry blonde hair seemed to shimmer until the bright fluorescents as she stood to greet me. "Asena Vasko, I'm one of the High Alphas."

I inclined my head, "Nice to meet you."

"I want to say, I am sorry for your loss. My son is just a few years older than you, I can't imagine how he would handle losing either of us." She laid a hand on my shoulder, "If you need assistance from the wolves for anything, don't hesitate to ask."

"Actually, that's one the reasons I wanted to meet, Fallon." Radley motioned for us to join him at the table. "I've taken over your mother's role as Mayor of Mercy Valley for now, but next year it will be time for a new election. If you're interested in continuing Agana's legacy, I want you to know we will happily support your campaign."

"I'm not even old enough to run," I couldn't stop the laugh that left me at the suggestion. "You're far more likely to convince one of my mates to take that on."

Archer stepped in. "Until our rule over the Dragons of the Occydent is fully established, we will not be concerned with any political aspirations. If you choose to run, we will happily support you."

"That is good to know." Radley said, suppressing a smile, "I am getting old, so I have no intention of continuing my time as Mayor. We can discuss who we should support for the role another time."

"Have you had a chance to look through the files?" Conri asked, changing the subject.

I shook my head, "No, but I should have time very soon."

"I just want to remind you that, if you find out who did this, please let us know. I understand that if it was... another Dragon, that its under your purview, but its important to all shifters that Mercy Valley is kept safe from crimes like this." He said.

I forced myself not to roll my eyes, even though I wanted nothing more than to roll them until they fell out of my head at his little speech. "The Dragons have worked to keep Mercy Valley safe for hundreds of years, my mother most of all. I will continue that legacy regardless of who dared to harm her."

"Speaking of, your mother used to be the one to greet all of the new shifters in Mercy Valley. While the Mayor would usually handle that duty, I feel it would be best if it stayed with the Dragon Queen." Radley said, "Are you willing to do that?"

I glanced at Marlow, whose excitement couldn't be contained, "Yes, of course. The Dragons intend to continue to play a vital role in shifter relations in Mercy Valley."

"That is great news!" Asena said. As she glanced to my wing, I saw the motherly concern pass across her face. "Now, we hate to keep you too long with that injured wing."

We all said our goodbyes and headed out of the diner the back way. As soon as Conri, Asena, and Radley left I looked at my mates, "That could have been an email."

Marlow snorted, "It's good to have a close relationship with the High Luna of the Wolves. They are the largest group of shifters in Mercy Valley."

"But we hold more power." Archer pointed out. "The Dragon Queens of the Occident have poured money and energy into this town for hundreds of years."

"Is one of us going to have to be Mayor one day?" Bain asked.

I shrugged as we walked through town. My wings were cloaked to human eyes, but every shifter turned to look as we passed. Some gave me respectful nods or pitying looks, but most glanced to the men that surrounded me and scurried away. I knew the people of Mercy Valley well. All shifters were weary of new, obviously powerful beasts roaming through their town, but knowing who I am only increased their interest... and their fear. New Kings could change Mercy Valley for the better... or the worst. Archer, Marlow, and Bain would have to prove themselves. The thought stopped me in my tracks.

"Would y'all like to meet the Dragons that live in Mercy Valley? They'll be your Clan very soon." I asked.

Marlow grinned, "I've been waiting for someone to ask."

Archer nodded, staring down at his phone, "It would be better to meet them before my mother arrives in a couple of days."

Bain looked hesitant. "Maybe I should wait until..." I could see him searching for an excuse, so I laid my hand on his arm, sending my love and my confidence in him through our bond. He relaxed slightly, but sighed, "Let's do it."

THE DRAGONS of Mercy Valley weren't as organized as some of the other shifter groups. For the most part, Dragon Clans were capable of governing themselves. The Queens existed to end squabbles between the Clans and ensure that the Dragons as a whole remained strong and unified. I'd been forced to sit through many lectures of the days before the Dragons were unified, when the world was new and chaos reigned. The world had been different then. The witches just starting to learn their powers. Vampires ruling over large swaths of Europe. Shifters of all creeds roamed and killed as they please.

Humans were prey in those times, but I'd never seen the appeal of eating them. Too fatty.

"Princess Fallon Eyre has arrived," A guard at the gate shouted, before bowing at the waist, "To what do we owe this honor?"

"The future Kings want to meet our Clan." I answered, gesturing toward my mates.

The guard's eyes widened, "Lady Mika will be out to greet you momentarily."

I held in a snort. Mika would hate that he'd called her by her official title. It was one of the reasons she'd been pissed when everyone had elected her as the representative of the Mercy Valley Clan.

She appeared, her long, black hair unkempt in a white dressing gown. I couldn't stop the grin as she approached me, the scent of sex and her mate's sea salt scent wafting through the air. "Good morning, Princess... Queen... What is it now?"

"I'll be your Queen next month, for now I'm still just Fallon." I responded.

"Thank God, I was hoping this wasn't an official visit. You know you're supposed to give me some noticed before you come." She complained, but I could see the fondness in her eyes. We'd been friends for years. Our mothers had been close until hers had passed away from old age a few years ago. Mika had spent a month in my home, under the guidance of my mom, when she found out that the Clan wanted her to become their Lady. She had hoped the title would pass to her cousin, but the Clan had spoken. Their beloved Mika had become Lady Tavara.

"What would the fun in that be?" I asked, "Maybe I just want to see my friend for the first time in months." I saw the pity flash in her eyes, and it was a blow to my ego, "Really I wanted to introduce my mates to the Mercy Valley Clan." I muttered.

Finally, Mika's eyes moved away from me, widening as she took in the three men looming behind me. "I didn't know the rumors were true. Three Kings?"

I nodded, "I always have to be different."

Mika moved past me, extending a hand to Archer first, "It's nice to meet you. I am Lady Mika Tavara, I'm the representative of the Dragons in Mercy Valley. We operate a bit differently than the other Clans, so you may find some of our people a bit... disrespectful."

"They have no real respect until you've proven yourself." I explained, "Once a year, the Dragons of Mercy Valley gather together and have a gladiator type fight. It determines everyone's job and ranking within the Clan."

"That seems... barbaric." Bain interjected, "So the weakest Dragons have the worst jobs."

Mika shook her head, "No no. The opposite actually, and none of the children or elders are involved. Just the able men and women of age. It's really just for fun now, a tradition of the old. Everyone had already chosen their place within the Clan. They just want bragging rights."

"Is Steven still mad about me beating him last year?" I asked.

"He still tells everyone you shouldn't be allowed to participate since you'll be Queen someday. Your power is an unfair advantage." Mika laughed, leading us through the gate.

"That's bullshit. I still haven't taken on the full power of the Queen. I won't until my coronation." I said, seconds before a heavy weight slams against my middle.

"Auntie Fall! You haven't visited in soooo long." Mika's daughter, Jael, said as she wrapped her tiny body around mine.

"You've grown so much. You're almost as big as I am." I responded, "Are you ten yet?"

"I'm only eight!" Jael responded, "I still can't fly in this form." She pouted.

"It takes time, baby dragon." I smoothed her black hair down, pressing a kiss to her temple. "Go tell the other kids I'm here." She grinned, rushing toward the compound that had just come into view.

Deep within the mountains, the first Dragon Queen had begun building Mercy Valley's first compound to keep her Clan safe. Now all the shifters had a version of this place. Shifters had greater power in numbers, that's why Mercy Valley had become such a hot spot over the centuries. I'd never get over the tall marble walls that protected the twenty-eight dragons that made up my Clan. Dragons had been dwindling in number for the last century, the Dragons of the Oryent had stronger numbers, but not by a lot. When my mother had only had one child, rumors had swirled that the Dragons of the Occydent were becoming weaker, would die out in a hundred years. But as I glanced toward Mika, I grinned, noticing the small bump she'd been concealing with her night gown.

"When will they hatch?" I whispered. Her eyes were wide, but she gave a sigh of relief, "I haven't told anyone but William. The egg should complete incubation next week. Then it takes about six weeks to hatch." She moved her night gown aside, revealing the black and purple scales of the egg that was nestled against her stomach. "I was tired of being stuck in my beast form. William made this so I could still do all of duties." Dragons could only have our eggs in our beast form, and it was expected that mothers would stay in beast form keeping the egg warm, until it hatched. "Congratulations." I muttered, running my fingers over the warm surface of the egg.

When we entered the compound, warmth wrapped around us like the building was welcoming us itself. Recognizing that we were its highest protectors, that I carried the blood of its creator in my body. I'd often wondered as a child if it was sentient in some way, but I'd found no proof of that aside from the feeling of home that it conjured up. I loved our home, lower down the mountain, but without my parents and Mateo it felt empty. My mates helped, but I wasn't sure if it would ever feel like home again.

We entered the cafeteria, twenty sets of eyes turning our way. "Our future Queen is here to introduce you to your new Kings. Try to remember how to behave, please." Mika said.

I waved to everyone. "I know I'll be seeing all of you at our coronation next month, but I feel it's very important that your Kings meet their Clan now. Let me introduce you to my mates." I motioned for Marlow first, "This is Marlow Faelor, the oldest son of the Scottish Faelor Clan." Marlow grinned and inclined his head in respect. "This is Prince Archer Dabel, seventh son of Queen Phaedra of the Oryent." A few people gasped as Archer gave a smirk and a wave, "And finally, Bainbridge Abasom. He was a member of the Hambridge Clan." Bain bowed slightly, but I could see the discomfort painted across his face as he righted himself. He didn't enjoy being the center of attention, but I had faith it was something he would overcome with time. Sadly, as the Queen and Kings of the Dragons of the Occydent, we wouldn't be able to completely avoid the spotlight. Starting out here, with our Clan, would at least help him get started.

"Eat, go about your morning. We will mingle in so that your Kings can meet everyone." I said, before beelining to the food line. My stomach rumbled with hunger as I realized we hadn't eaten all day.

Before I could grab my tray, one of the elders approached me. "Princess Fallon, I wanted to come and give you, my condolences. Your parents were so good to all of us."

"Thank you. I hope my mates and I can continue their legacy." I said.

Our day continued much the same way. Everyone came to me to give their condolences and congratulations. Archer impressed a group of men by producing his fire in human form, Bain grinned as children crawled all over him, and Marlow chatted with everyone as if he'd known them his entire life. I just watched my Clan and my mates, my heart swelling with love and pride.

In that moment I realized something that changed everything. My grief would never go away, but I could fill my life with love and joy. It was the only way I could honor myself and my parents. My mates deserved that and so did every Dragon that I would rule over.

My bed was covered in the police report that Conri had given me. Every scrap of evidence the police had found, every interview with a witness... every single detail they'd managed to find. Yet... It was nothing. No one had seen the shooter, just my mother's body dropping to the ground, blood pooling all around her body. I yanked my eyes away from that photo, unable to stomach another moment of staring at it.

"Fallon, I'm coming in." Marlow's voice startled me. I'd sent my mates away late last night, knowing I needed to do this alone. I considered trying to hide the evidence of my insanity, but he didn't give me a chance. "Have ye slept at all?" I cringed as he took in my face. I was still in the clothes I'd been wearing last night, my hair thrown into a messy bun. I glanced in the mirror of my vanity, noting the dark bags under my golden eyes.

"I'll rest later. I've got to look over all of this." I tried to wave him off.

"Nay. Nay." Marlow shook his head, scooping me into his arms, "Queen Phaedra could arrive at any time. I'm taking you to my room to sleep."

"I can't rest until I know who did this, Low." I cried as he carried me from my room.

"I'll look over it all while you sleep. Maybe you need fresh eyes on it." He said. He kicked open the door to the room he'd been sleeping in, dropping me unceremoniously onto the bed.

When he turned to leave, I whispered, "Stay?"

"For my angel, always." He crawled in next to me, letting me curl into his side, and rest my head against his wide chest. "Archer, Bain, and I are here to help you, Fallon. Once you fall asleep, all three of us will look at those files. See what we can figure out."

"Thank you," I muttered, finally letting sleep take me.

INCESSANT KNOCKING BROUGHT me out of my sleep. "What? What?" I shouted, groggily.

"Ma'am, I'm here to get you ready. Prince Archer sent me. Queen Phaedra has arrived." A small female voice was muffled by the door.

"Fuck." I muttered, throwing the covers off of my body. "Come in."

The woman that stepped into the room was clearly nervous. She was taller than me by several inches, but had her body hunched over in deference. She was clearly one of the people that had been accompanying Archer since his arrival. "I have a bath drawn and your clothes laid out in your room, Princess Fallon."

"What's your name?" I asked as I let her lead me back to my own room.

"Ruby, Princess." She said. I took her in, noting the brown wings and deep orange eyes she had. She was a pretty young girl, and I wondered how she had ended up working for Archer.

"What am I wearing to meet the Queen of the Oryent, Ruby?" I made my voice as light as possible, not wanting to make her afraid.

"Prince Archer selected a gown from your closet. He said it would complement what he and your other mates would be wearing." She responded.

"Will you be staying with Archer after we have bonded?" I asked, as I disrobed to climb into the tub.

Ruby kept her eyes averted, respectfully, "Yes, Princess. I am the only person who will remain with Prince Archer after his mother leaves."

"Why you?" I asked.

I glanced to see that her eyes had widened, discomfort clear in her stance, "I am no threat to you, Princess. I have been a maid to Prince Archer for two years now."

"Not just a maid though," I observed, "There's a knife stashed in your boot. While you are uncomfortable with me and clearly doing your best to be respectful, your body shows the signs. You're more bodyguard than maid."

Her shock was evident, an actual gleam of respect in her eye, "You're far more keen than I was led to believe. Yes, I spent five years training under Queen Phaedra's mate, Kaizen, to be part of the guard. Prince Archer was assigned to me when he began to travel for work. Now, I will stay with him."

"Happy to have you as part of the family." I said, as I finished my bath. Ruby handed me a towel.

"Take a seat. I can do your hair, while you do your makeup." She instructed after I had dried off, and dressed in a bra and panties. We worked quickly, I brushed dark red lipstick over my lips, a shade that almost perfectly matched my hair. I appreciated that it shimmered like wet blood, it felt appropriate to meet Queen Phaedra. I was nervous. The way Archer spoke, made me expect Queen Phaedra to be even more uptight than he was. I wanted to make a good impression. The Oryent and Occydent Dragons would be bond in a new way. It could open doors for our species that had been closed for far too long. Ruby had carefully piled my hair so that it fell down my back in loose waves, black gems shining from the pins she'd used. She handed me the gown, and I couldn't help the grin that spread over my face. It had been custom made for me, the silk was the same color as my eyes. Every brush of it over my skin was heaven. The back was open, allowing for me to really show off my wings.

"Damn," I whispered as I looked in the mirror, "Not sure it's appropriate to meet my mother in law, but Archer has great taste."

Ruby snorted, "They are waiting for you in the throne room."

I walked purposefully downstairs, grinning as Marlow and Bain greeted me. They were dressed in matching suits. Only Bain's was pure black, while Marlow's was a deep, royal blue. "Ye look stunning, angel."

"Like a true Queen." Bain said, pressing a kiss to my hand as he took it.

"Let's hope Queen Phaedra approves," I muttered as they led me to the door.

Ruby stepped ahead of us, announcing our arrival. "Princess Fallon and her mates Marlow Faelor and Bainbridge Abasom." Bain cringed as they announced his full name but had his face righted as we swept into the room. I ignored my grief as I noticed the room was bustling with Queen Phaedra's people, but only Uncle Adam was familiar to me. My fathers should have been here. I shook my head, focusing on the room.

It didn't take much to find Queen Phaedra. She sat on a makeshift throne in the center of the room. Her black hair brushed the ground around her, and a small silver tiara sat atop her brow. Her wings were out, relaxing against the chair, the shimmering pale blue color stark against her perfect creamy skin. I curtsied as I approached her, "Queen Phaedra, welcome to my home. It's an honor to have you." Her facial expression betrayed nothing as her red eyes roved over me. I straightened, "I'm so glad you were able to join Prince Archer and I for our bonding ceremony."

The older Queen stood, and began to circle me, forcing my mates to move further away from me. I didn't flinch, tuning out the slow click of her heels. I was on edge when she stopped inches from me.

She tilted my chin down, "Your mother often bragged about how beautiful you had become. I'm happy to see she was not lying to make me jealous."

"Thank you." I breathed, "My mother often spoke highly of you. I hope as I take my place as Queen we can continue the relationship of respect you shared with her."

For the first time, a small smile broke across her face. "The bond between the Queens of the Occydent and Oryent is vital to the continuation of our species." She leaned in, "The Occydent and Oryent will be even closer once your bond with Archer is complete."

As if summoned by his name, Archer stepped into the room. Every eye turned to take in the deep green suit that he wore. His wings nearly blended with its color, but what drew my eyes were the golden accents he'd selected. A perfect match to my dress. "Mother, I hope you aren't aiming to intimidate my mate."

Queen Phaedra rolled her eyes, waving off the servants, "Leave us. It is time I get to know the Clan my son will be ruling over." Everyone began to file out of the room instantly. Once we were alone, she said, "Please tell me we have somewhere more comfortable to chat than these thrones."

I couldn't stop the laugh that bubbled out of me, "Why the hell are they so uncomfortable?"

"To force you to think about your posture. God forbid the Clans see their Queen as anything other than perfectly poised." She responded, before turning to Archer, "Well... Is that all that greeting your mother gets?"

"It's good to see you, Mom. It's been too long." Archer said, stooping down to hug her.

"I told you to ignore your father, and stay in my court, but you insisted on trapezing around the world." Phaedra chided, "Now, I'm famished. Do I have to go hunt my own food while I'm here?"

Marlow laughed, "While I'm sure ye could teach us a lot about hunting, Archer has prepared us a meal to share."

"You're cooking again?" She asked with surprise, before turning to me, "I hope you continue to influence him to do what he actually enjoys."

Archer's cheeks had flushed a deep red, but I could see the love he had for his mother in his eyes. I grinned, "I'm so glad you could come."

"WHEN ARCHER WAS SIX, before his wings were strong enough to carry him, he had Kaizen and his father, Lionel, stressed beyond belief. He'd climb up on any high surface he could find and jump trying to fly." Phaedra threw her head back and laughed. "You never get the image of your naked six-year-old jumping from the top banister of stairs trying to catch wind with his tiny wings. I thought Lionel was going to have a stroke."

"He still claims I was the one who turned him grey," Archer mumbled.

"You can't deny you have pulled your fair share of stunts." She responded, tossing back the last of the wine in her glass.

I was buzzed and contented. Queen Phaedra had completely shocked me. While I could see why Archer was uptight and duty-focused, it was nice to see a more relaxed side of him. Being the youngest son of the Dragon Queen was not an easy life, especially when your oldest siblings are pushing a hundred years old.

"I think that's enough fun for one night." Archer said, standing, "After all, Fallon needs her rest. We're bonding day after tomorrow."

I snorted, glancing toward his Mother, "Is he always such a buzz kill?"

"He's a good boy... Or well... He is now." Phaedra laughed, "But I will be heading to bed myself. I promised everyone that we would go explore Mercy Valley tomorrow."

"I'm going with her to make sure they don't have any trouble." Archer explained as he escorted me to my bedroom door.

I leaned up, pressing a kiss to his cheek, "I'll see you when it's time to bond."

The lust in his eyes nearly knocked me off my feet, and I glanced back finding Queen Phaedra averting her eyes with a knowing smile. I hadn't expected to be fond of her; she had always seemed so intimidating when my mother talked about her. Even more from Archer, but I could see that she was far more down to earth than anyone gave her credit for. A blessing that she did not instantly hate me.

"Goodnight, Princess Fallon." She laid a hand on my shoulder, giving me a loving squeeze before Archer escorted her away.

Marlow and Bain followed me into my room, and I gasped. All of the police files had been moved off of my bed and hung on a brand-new board on the wall. "You did all of this while I slept?" I asked, tears filling my eyes.

"I wish you'd told us more about what ye were doing." Marlow chided, "I could have been helping ye from day one. Come here, I want to show you something."

Bain stopped me, handing me a set of cream colored, silk pajamas, "Change first."

I yanked the dress over my head, and shed my bra instantly, pulling the clothes on quickly before rushing to Marlow's side. He opened his fist, revealed a small, silver casing. His skin smoked slightly from the contact, but he ignored it, "This is the bullet that shot you." He jabbed a finger at a photo from the crime scene, "It has the same etching on the side as the ones that killed your mother."

"We already knew it had to be the same person." I sighed.

"Yes, but we know it was the same gun now. And that's not all." Marlow said, pulling down a photo and a page of the report, "Yer mother was shot in the back, three times. It was close range. I think she knew whoever killed her, enough to turn her back on them."

"How did no one see anything if the person was with her?" I paced the floor, "It doesn't make any sense."

"I don't know. There's some sort of spell work involved. I've never been keen on the witches, so I can't give ye more information right now." He sighed, "I'm sorry I didn't find more."

I shook my head, "No. If it was obvious, I would have figured it out by now." I pulled him down for a kiss, soaking in the warmth of his body, "The fact you've tried this much means the world to me... I love you."

"I love ye too, pet. I couldn't have been blessed with a better mate." He kissed me fiercely for several minutes, before pulling away, and directing me to Bain. "And I've been blessed with the bonds of brotherhood."

Bain wrapped his arms around me, our bond buzzing with his happiness at Marlow's words, "I never imagined when Hambridge came here that I would find a family... I am so glad I did."

"I love you." I whispered as I kissed him softly.

"I've never loved anyone before, Fallon, but you are the sun that brightens my day. Every time I open my eyes, and feel you in my mind... in my heart... I am overcome. There is nothing I would not do to show you just how much I adore you." Bain said, causing tears to fill my eyes again. These men... who had been in my life for such a short period of time had done everything they could to ease my burden. My mates, with their own pain and damage, had already shown me that they would put me first. I hoped that I could be everything they had dreamed a mate could be.

I sipped a cup of coffee as I stared at the wall covered in my mother's case file. Every detail and image swam in my mind. My eyes were blurry from barely blinking as I tried to see something I had missed. There was nothing; whoever had killed my mother had left no trace of themselves behind. Even a motive was beyond me at this point. With a huff, I picked up my phone. I was tired of not knowing where to look next. I opened my conversation with Willow and typed a quick sentence.

> You were right. I need to talk to my mother.

Her response was almost instant, as if she'd been waiting for me to text her.

Thank God. I'm ready to go back to
Oregon. I'll see you tonight.

I THREW myself down on my bed. Everyone was busy, so I had some time to actually relax, but as I stared up at the ceiling, I realized I didn't know what to do with myself. The grief, depression, and responsibilities of being a princess had robbed me of my hobbies and freedom for months. I stood, glancing around the room. When I noticed the book I'd purchased when Bain and I had gone on our first courting date, I grinned. I grabbed it and curled back up in bed.

The day turned to night in the blink of an eye as I lost myself in magic and romance. The story was captivating and deliciously naughty. Filling my mind with all sorts of ideas to try with my mates. So far, all of our encounters had been separate, but after Archer and I bonded tomorrow, I had hope they would be willing to do more.

A tap on my window drew me from my horny musings. Willow stood on my balcony, her short black hair blowing in the wind. I opened the door, allowing her inside.

"We need a table to do this." She said in lieu of greeting. I led her into my sitting room, motioning to the table at the center of my seating arrangement. We didn't speak as she went to work, setting up black-and-white candles at each of the four corners. She lit them, and while no words left her mouth, a chill began to fill the room. "Sit." She commanded me once she had finished placing a small selection of gems in the center of the table. She laid her hands on the table face up, revealing her tattooed palms. I tried to look closer at the strange rune-like symbols, but she grabbed my hands, forcing me to look into her haunting grey eyes. "Think of your mother, the very best memories you have of her. Picture her in your mind," Willow instructed. "Close your eyes if it makes it easier."

I followed her instruction, conjuring one of my favorite memories to the front of my mind. My mother was wearing her favorite plum colored pant suit. We strolled down Main Street, arm in arm, laughing as snow fell around us. It melted as soon as it touched our skin due to Dragon's hot nature, but we still tried to catch snowflakes in our open mouths. She was talking about her next meeting with the Coyotes, and her hopes of finally brokering peace between them and the Wolves. I admired her passion and drive, but she turned to me, a serious look on her face. "Fallon, I know you're young right now, but one day these problems will lay on your shoulders." I nodded, sensing that she was telling me something important. "I hope I am by your side when you take the throne, as my mother had been for me, but if I am not... I want you to know that I am so proud of the woman you're becoming. You will make a great Queen one day."

A tear rolled down my face. I hadn't thought of that conversation in years.

"I was right, ya know." My eyes popped open at my Mother's voice filled the room. In the center of the table, between mine and Willow's joined hands, a translucent image of my Mother's face had appeared. She looked just as she had the last time, I'd seen her alive. Red hair braided back from her face, deep brown eyes so full of warmth.

"Oh, momma." I cried, tears streaming down my face. "I'm so sorry. I should have been here. I should never have snuck out."

"My baby..." She cooed, "My perfect Fallon. You are young, you didn't do anything wrong. You could not have stopped this from happening. If it hadn't been that night, it would have happened another time." She sighed, "I made enemies in my reign. No one appreciates someone shooting down what they want."

"Do you know who killed you?" Willow asked. I took in her face, sweat pouring from her hair line. Her skin paler than usual, bags had developed under her eyes already. She looked ill, but squeezed my hands, bringing my attention back to my mother's ghost.

My mother hummed, brows knitting together, "That night is fuzzy. The last thing I remember is a phone call from Adam about his newest idea for the Clan's investments. I was leaving the store…" She trailed off, "I'm sorry. I don't know anything else."

Willow groaned, "I'm sorry, Fallon. I can't hold this connection open much longer. She's just too powerful."

My vision was blurry as I stared into my mother's face, trying to memorize every line, "I love you, Mom. I'm going to find whoever did this and then I'm going to be the best Queen the Dragons of the Occydent have ever seen. I swear."

"Be yourself, Fallon. That is all that the Clans need from you. I already know you'll be amazing. I raised you after all." She smiled, "Let those fine mates of yours take care of you. Your fathers are sending all of their love. We will see you in the next life." Her voice came distant as her face began to flicker out of existence.

"I can't wait." I whispered, as the candles blew out. Willow crashed backwards, and I rushed to her side, using my beast's strength to lift her onto the couch. Her skin was freezing. I reached for a blanket, but threw it aside, summoning warmth from my core. I'd noticed my powers growing for weeks. But as red scales rippled over my hands, my hands heating instantly I knew my transformation into the Queen of the Occydent wasn't far off. I laid my hands over her chest and stomach, willing my heat into her slowly. For several minutes, there was no change, but eventually her skin returned to its usual color. I sat by her side in silence until she finally woke up.

She bolted up, frantically, "What… Oh…" She sighed, "Sorry. It's harder to channel the spirits of the supernatural. Human souls are easy, but your mother… She was powerful."

I laid a hand on her shoulder, squeezing slightly, "Thank you. It means a lot to get one last moment with her."

She brushed me off, standing, "I'm going to head back home tonight."

"Before you go," I grabbed my purse, producing several high bills, "Take this. I know you're struggling up there."

"I don't take payment for my abilities." Willow snapped.

"Take it as a gift from a friend... or as payment for your travel expenses." I demanded, shoving the money into her hand, "If you ever need anything... You've got my number."

She didn't say another word, stepping out onto the balcony and disappearing in the blink of an eye. I watched the spot for a long time, wondering if I'd ever see Willow Ashcroft again. She'd helped me more than I'd actually expected her to. The hole in my heart was slowly stitching back up, and I owed a small piece of that to the girl haunted by ghosts.

"You really should eat breakfast, Princess." Ruby said as she brushed through my hair, "You won't be able to eat until after the ceremony if you don't."

I just shook my head slightly. I was nervous. Bonding with Archer would be different than bonding with Marlow or Bain. Not only would our bonding be witnessed by everyone... Archer and I were closer, but there was still a wall between us. It would disappear today, whether we were ready or not. Not to mention that it was the final step before I could take the throne. I gulped, "Is everything ready?"

Ruby nodded, "Queen Phaedra's team has taken care of everything. Lady Mika sent a message that she'd be attending in her official capacity as well."

That made me feel strangely better. Without my parents, the only people who would be there for me were Uncle Adam and my other mates. At least if Mika was there, I'd feel less alone. Bonding with my final mate cemented my coronation date, and I couldn't wrap my mind around it. Was I truly prepared to be Queen?

"We are ready." My beast rumbled in the back of my mind, *"The power of the Queen has already taken root. As soon as we are recognized by the Clans, we can take our rightful place."*

I sighed. Even my beast had more confidence than I did. I couldn't even figure out who had killed my mother... or why. How was I going to lead half a race of Dragons?

A quiet knock on the door interrupted my spiraling thoughts. Queen Phaedra swept in, already dressed in swaths of green and gold. "Ruby, can you leave us alone for a moment?" She nodded, bowing to us both before slipping out the door. I stood, allowing the black dress I wore to fall to the floor. "You look gorgeous, Princess. My son is extremely lucky."

"Thank you, Your Majesty." I inclined my head.

"Oh, stop it with all of that." She said, sitting down on the bed. She patted the space next to her, "Sit. In just under an hour, you will bond with my son. While I respect that you may not feel comfortable with it now, I expect you to call me Phaedra eventually. For the first time, the Dragons will be ruled by a single-family unit. I think that calls for more celebration than you can truly comprehend." She took my hand, "I can't stay for your coronation, but I want you to know that the Dragons of the Oryent stand by your side."

"Thank you... Phaedra." I said with a soft smile. "I'll admit I was terrified to meet you."

She laughed, "I'm sure Archer didn't help one bit. He was always such a serious child. I'm glad he gave up the businesses to focus on his mate."

"He gave them up?" The way he'd explained it, I'd assumed that decision had been made by his family.

"Oh... Yes, he called and talked to his father weeks ago. Asked him to redistribute everything but the restaurants." Queen Phaedra revealed. He'd given up all the businesses he'd been working on for years... for me. "Your Uncle is going to come walk you down when it's time for the ceremony to begin." I had missed most of what she said, absorbed in this new reality. Archer... He had chosen our life together over his duty to his family.

I sat, letting my mind drift off to imagine the life ahead of me for a moment. In less than a month, I'd be Queen of the Occident Dragons. My mates would be Kings. We would rule over twenty Clans, the faces of a new era for the Dragons. I'd spent time this week pouring over my mother's journals, reading about all that she had managed to change and implement in her time on the throne. She'd nearly ended all servitude contracts, had brokered peace among so many shifters in Mercy Valley, and even made Clan investments that had made the Dragons even richer. I had ideas floating around, images of a world where all the Dragon Clans shared their resources, where new Clans arose, and new hatchlings were born every day. I knew finding mates had become difficult for many of the younger dragons. I wanted to change that. My mates had saved my life. Every dragon deserved to experience that. With Phaedra as my ally, I could create a matchmaking service for the Dragons. Maybe even expand it to other shifters in the future. Mercy Valley was the perfect testing ground for that kind of idea.

A knock on the door drew my attention to the present day. I stood, smoothing my dress into place. I knew I looked good; I had no doubts as I strode to the door. Uncle Adam smirked, "Ready to be bonded off?"

I took his arm, allowing him to lead me to the throne room one last time. After this I'd never have to be separated from my mates. We could finally share rooms without being concerned about the optics. Soon, I'd call the staff and Clan members back home. I missed having the halls bustling with people. It'd been too silent for too long.

As we entered the room, my breath rushed out of my body. It had been transformed, the throne was gone, in its place was a covered area. I knew a bed was behind it, so that we could complete our bonding. Queen Phaedra and Lady Mika stood side by side on the raised area. My eyes went straight to Archer. He stood below them in tight black pants and a green button down. Like me he was barefoot. Uncle Adam led to my waiting mate, giving me a kiss on the cheek before joining the small audience that was here to witness their Princess bond.

"Welcome, I am Queen Phaedra Dabel of the Oryent Dragons. Prince Archer is my son, and I am here to witness his bonding ceremony to Princess Fallon Eyre. This is an exciting mating ceremony, and I cannot thank the fates enough for bringing us together today." She took a deep breath. "Let us join the Dragons together, through the bond that Archer and Fallon will cement today."

Lady Mika stepped forward, giving me a small wink before she said. "Unfortunately, Queen Agana Eyre of the Occydent Dragons is not here to witness her daughters bonding. I am here as a representative of our Clan, but also as a friend to Princess Fallon. Let us celebrate the strong bond between mates."

Archer took my hands, "Princess Fallon Agana Eyre, will you complete our mate bond and allow me to rule by your side?"

"I will." I breathed out. "Prince Archer Kaizen Dabel, will you complete our mate bond, and rule over the Dragon Clans of the Occydent with me?"

"It would be my honor." He said, leaning in to press his lips to mine. My beast pushed forward, wrapped in the golden light of mates, she reached into Archer's mind directly to his beast who was waiting. As they met, golden light in the shape of our beasts surrounded us. Our bond pulsed in the air. I had to squeeze my thighs together to avoid wrapping myself around my mate.

"Archer and Fallon will now complete their bond." I couldn't tell who spoke, their voices were far away as Archer nearly dragged me toward the sparkling black curtains. We slipped inside, and all the noise that had filled the room moments before completely faded away.

"I don't want to rip that dress, but I need you to be naked... Now." He rumbled. I laughed as I yanked the fabric away from my overheated skin. He was naked before I had fully disrobed. He was on me in an instant, hands exploring every inch of my body with a desperation I wasn't expecting. When he cupped my pussy, I moaned, grinding against his palm, "This belongs to me now, just like the rest of you." He sunk his teeth into my neck as he prodded my entrance with a finger, "And look you're so wet and ready for me."

"Please, Archer." I groaned, "I want you to fuck me." His red eyes were glowing with the power of his beast as he lifted my body dropping me down onto his cock in a single move. I screamed out as we connected, stars flashing in my eyes. He pounded into me with a wild rhythm, grunting with every thrust. I noticed tears in his eyes and couldn't stop myself from wiping them away. "I'm sorry our courting hasn't been easy, but I never want you to doubt that I... I love you." As soon as the words left my mouth, Archer lost all sense of control. He dropped my body down to the mattress, holding my hips up high and punishing me with his cock. I was split open and lost in pleasure when he finally groaned his release. The feeling of his hot seed filling me was enough to push me over the edge. Golden light snapped around us one more time, before I felt him in my mind.

"You'll never be able to hide anything from me again." I whispered into his mind.

"I don't want to." He responded, pressing a kiss to my lips as he carefully pulled away. "We have to rejoin the party now."

Archer helped me back into my dress, before pulling his clothes back on. "I'm so glad my cum is going to dripping down your thighs for the rest of the night." He muttered into my ear just before we emerged.

Everyone clapped and cheered, but my cheeks filled with heat at Archer's dirty words. I wanted to drag him back to my room, but Bain and Marlow were by my side before I could voice the words. Marlow wrapped me in a hug first, "We are finally one unit."

Bain clapped Archer on the back, "Welcome to the family, Archie."

"No. Do not call me that." Archer growled.

I noted the sparkle of mischief in Bain's eyes, and grinned. My mates had already started to form a brotherhood, and now I was finally bonded to all of them. Things were finally looking up. The Dragons of the Occydent would be ruled by a Queen and her Kings that were truly united.

I SCREAMED as Marlow forced a fourth orgasm out of me. My body shook, and I collapsed back onto my bed, panting and spent. When he ran his fingers gently over my pussy, I begged, "Low, please. It's... It's been two hours. I can't take anymore."

"Ye'll take whatever I give you, pet." He said, "But, mercy for now. I know ye've got things to do today."

He was right. Queen Phaedra had left yesterday, insisting that the Dragons of the Oryent just couldn't function any longer without her. I think Archer was relieved that she'd taken everyone but Ruby with her.

"Have you heard from your mother? Is Clan Faelor going to be represented at our coronation?" I asked as I climbed into the shower.

"She called yesterday. She and my sister will be here to pledge their fealty." He said, "And six other Clans have confirmed their attendance. Archer is sending out letters, emails, and I swear I saw him with a Raven shifter yesterday." I shook my head. We were all running around, ensuring the coronation was perfect. At least I didn't have to do it alone. "I've got to go into town, pick up a few groceries and... A few other things." Marlow's cheeks were pink, and

I had a feeling whatever he was planning to pick up was a surprise for me.

"Sounds good. Bain is out flying; Archer took Ruby into town to get things for the new room. I'm just going to work." I kissed his cheek, "Dinner tonight at six!" I shouted as I headed to the office.

***

I GROANED as I stretched my back. I'd been stooped over the desk for hours, working through the backlog of paperwork that had been building up. I'd finally gotten it caught up, but as I wandered through the house, I realized no one had gotten home yet. When my stomach rumbled, I decided to see if Uncle Adam was home and whether I could enjoy some lunch. As I approached his door, I heard the sounds of raised voices.

"You can't be serious, Amaya. Your father said you could give me the fucking spell. Give it to me." Adam's voice was muffled, but his shouting could easily be heard. "His spell worked well enough for my sister, but I need death magic for my niece."

My heart stopped in my chest, but my beast was already pushing forward, processing what he'd said faster than I could. She took over our body in an instant. I kicked through the door, rage clouding my vision. "It was you." I growled, more beast than anything, "You killed my mother. You shot me." Adam's brown eyes were wide as I approached him, my hands morphing into talons and scales. "Admit it!" I shouted. Tears had blurred my vision, so I couldn't prepare as he flew at me. A sharp pain in my neck was the last thing I felt before I fell into darkness.

I GROANED as I came back into consciousness. My neck and back ached, but I didn't have time to worry about that. I opened my eyes to dim lights in an unfamiliar room. The walls were wooden paneled, a small bed was set to my left. I couldn't see much else. As I tried to move, I realized I was tied to the chair. When I couldn't break out of the ropes myself, I reached for my beast, but she was gone. Asleep. Panic clawed at my throat, until I remembered the bonds that now lived lodged in my mind. I brushed along my connection to my mates, reaching for them. Without my beast, the feelings were fuzzy, some concern and fear buzzed down the bond, but I couldn't hear any words. I tried to send images... Adam. Adam...

My uncle had killed my mother; had been planning to try to kill with death magic. I shook my beast in my mind to no avail. Without her awake I was locked away from all of my power. I was trapped, unsure if Marlow, Bain, or Archer had understood any of what I had tried to convey. I was trapped, unsure what my uncle had planned.

I heard a door open behind me, and I stiffened as Adam walked into my vision. "You bastard." I growled, "I'll fucking end you for this."

He had the audacity to laugh, "Fallon, you're tied to a chair, locked away from your Dragon, and completely at my mercy. Maybe you should try humbling yourself for once."

Rage boiled in my gut, so I spat in his face. He backhanded me, causing my lip to split and blood to flood my mouth. I spat on the ground, my chest rumbling with a primal noise I'd never heard before. "Why? Just tell me why you did it."

"Being the second born son of a Queen did me no favors. I was more qualified for the throne than Agana ever was. I had made the Clan hundred of thousands of dollars, all she cared about was the shifter community. Every idea I came to her with she shot down." He ranted, "Do you know the last thing she said to me before I shot her?" Adam laughed harshly, "She told me I had to stop bothering her with my silly pyramid schemes. Agana always treated me less than."

Money. He'd killed my mother because she wouldn't give him any more money. Rage rose in me, but with nowhere to go my grief rose with it. For weeks, my mother's killer had lived in my home, and I had done nothing to avenge her.

"That's bullshit," I finally snapped, "I've looked over the books. Every penny she gave you saw no return. My Dad was the investment guru, he made our Clan rich."

"And that's why you're here, my stupid little niece. You're just like her. You refuse to listen to reason. With you out of the way, I can become King of the Dragons of the Occydent. I can finally fix everything Agana broke." He said. "The problem is, I'm all out of bullets after I missed my chance to kill you a few weeks ago. And that bitch of a witch, Amaya, refused to give me the death spell I needed. So, get comfortable, Fallon. You'll be here until I can find a way to get rid of you."

I snorted, "Not powerful enough to even kill yourself. You hide behind witch's spells and guns." I saw the hit coming this time, and I laughed as more blood flooded my mouth, "You're pathetic."

He stormed out of the room, and I sighed. Until my Dragon awoke, there was nothing I could do but pray that he didn't find a way to end my life. Pray that my mates would find me.

"*WAKE UP,*" I begged, laying a mental hand on my Dragon. Begging her to return. It had been hours, my entire body ached from the drugs and being held in the same position for so long. *"Please. I need you."* I felt tears roll down my face, but there was nothing I could do. I had trusted my Uncle, had never suspected that it could have been him. But as I considered it, the signs had been there. I'd let my mother's killer live in my house, give me over to my mate. The betrayal stung. I had no family left.

"We have our mates, and we don't want that scum as our family anyway." My beasts voice floated through my mind, causing me to sob with relief. *"I'm still weak, but the longer he takes to come back the more ready I'll be."*

"What is the plan?" I asked.

My beast chuffed, *"I'm going to burn him to ash."* I wasn't sure it would be that easy, but I didn't have space for doubt. I would have to be ready the moment he returned. Bid my time carefully, until I could free myself from him.

The minutes ticked by, turning into hours. It was impossible to tell how long I'd been here. My bonds were still fuzzy, barely reachable. Whatever drugs he'd injected me with, still hadn't faded from my system. When the door opened again, I stayed still. Adam stepped into my vision, opening his mouth to say something, but the fire had already been building in my core. A stream of blue fire rushed from my lips. He dived out of the way, but I could already see the damage on his face. Dragons may be heat resistant, but a Queen's fire was nothing like the rest. My beast tried to transform our hands, but it was impossible with the drugs in my system. Instead, I used my fire to burn away the ropes. I fell to my knees with a shout as my body moved for the first time in so long. I could barely move, but Adam's screaming had stopped. I knew I had to move before he gained the upper hand. I forced myself to my feet, ignoring the screaming of every inch of my body. I stumbled toward Adam, trying to summon more fire.

"I'm tapped out. Run!" My beast panted. I hesitated for just a moment, staring at my Uncle's half burned face as he crawled toward me.

"You'll never get away, Fallon. I'm going to take everything from you." He screamed, as I turned on my heel and busted out the door.

It was dark, impossible to see for a human, but I could see enough to stare up at the towering trees. I couldn't fly, I couldn't shift. I had to rely on my wobbling legs to get away. I picked a direction and ran, ignoring the sticks and stones that cut my feet. I ran blindly, praying and begging to find my way somewhere safe.

When strong arms wrapped around my middle, yanking me to a stop I screamed, flailing and hitting with every ounce of power that I had. "Pet, it's me. It's Marlow. I'm here. I've got ye. Bain and Archer are with me. Yer safe." Marlow's accent was thicker with his panic, but it soothed me. I sobbed, wrapping my arms around his neck.

"Adam. It was Adam. He-he..."

"We know." Archer growled, "We parsed out what we could through the bond. Where is he?"

"There's a cabin that way. I burned him, but he was still..."

Bain growled, taking off with his wings before I could finish my sentence. Archer was hot on his heels. Marlow kissed my head, "Thank God, yer okay. I did nay know what I was going to do if he hurt ye."

I couldn't speak anymore, sobs and emotions overwhelming me. Marlow just held me, allowing me to cry and scream my rage and grief into his chest. When Bain and Archer returned, I could see the truth in their eyes, "He got away."

Archer inclined his head. "I've already informed all the shifters in Mercy Valley and the surrounding Clans to keep an eye out. We'll come back tomorrow, hunt for clues, but we need to take you home. Now."

I nodded, allowing them to fly me home. Marlow took me straight into a hot bath, before Bain carefully cleaned and cared for the wounds on my feet. Archer hovered, his eyes switching between my face and his cell phone every few seconds. He typed furiously, and I knew he was working to unravel every piece of Adam's life. My mates wouldn't allow him to harm me so long as I was with them.

"Please don't leave me alone again." I whispered as Marlow tucked me into bed.

"You're lucky I'm not putting a tracker in your neck." Archer growled as he climbed in next to me. Marlow tucked into my other side, before Bain followed behind him.

"One of us will be with ye every moment for the rest of yer life." Marlow said, before pressing a kiss to my head, "Now sleep. We will watch over ye."

The warmth of my mates lulled me into sleep, but my dreams turned to nightmares. Visions of Adam shooting my mother, killing my mates... My uncle had destroyed my life once. I would find a way to stop him... Forever.

I awoke surrounded by warm bodies. It had become my
normal over the last week. During the day, one of the guys stayed
with me, whether I was resting, working, or milling around town. At
night, we all piled into my bed to sleep. Sadly, sleep was all I'd
managed to convince them to do each night. This morning was going
to be different. I shimmied my clothes off under the covers before
crawling between Archer's legs. His eyes opened the moment I
moved, taking in my nakedness. He didn't even hesitate to strip off
his pants, revealing his already hard cock. I pounced on him, sucking
him greedily.

Marlow stirred first, taking in the scene before him. He froze.
Archer gave him a slight nod, an invitation that I was desperate for.
He moved, palming his hardening cock through his pants, as he
crawled behind me. He pushed my legs apart roughly before his
tongue delved into my entrance. I moaned around Archer's cock,
bobbing in time with Marlow's licks. When he prodded my ass, I
nearly came undone, pressing back.

The noise woke Bain, who sat up, watching with wide eyes as the scene before him. I pulled away from Archer, "I need all of you. Please stay, fill my holes. I'm so empty without you."

"Such a dirty little pet," Marlow growled. "Bain, come here. Play with her pussy, while I open her ass up. She's going to take all of us today."

"I want her ass." Bain rumbled. We all glanced at him in shock, but Marlow agreed, returning his attention to my throbbing pussy. Bain's fingers were thicker than Marlow's, and the feel of him stretching me open was obscene. Archer reached down, playing with my nipples, as I gagged on his thick cock. The sensations were enough to push me over the edge; my orgasm caused my toes to curl and tingle. None of them let up, as my legs shook and I moaned around Archer's cock.

"She's ready." I was lifted as the men adjusted their positions. Archer stood at the end of the bed, cock wet from my spit and proudly bobbing. Marlow lay on the bed, turning me toward Archer, before pulling me down until he bumped into my cervix. Lights already danced behind my eyes, but Bain gave me no time to adjust, pressing into my ass slowly.

Archer grabbed my hair, forcing me to swallow every inch of him. They found a punishing rhythm, and my thoughts flooded away. I was completely filled by my mates. Every thrust was exquisite sensation. I never wanted the moment to end, wanted to live stuffed full of my mates until I died.

"Our. Good. Little. Mate." Bain slammed into my ass, and I felt his cum fill me. Marlow groaned, following closely behind him.

Archer pulled away from my mouth, "Beg, brat. Tell me what you want."

"Please fuck my throat," I cried out. Marlow was stuffing his fingers into both of my holes, as Bain slowly rubbed my clit, "Please, I need your cum Archer."

He grabbed my hair viciously, "Open wide, and take every fucking inch. You don't need air; you only need my cum." He slammed into my throat as tears and spit ran down my face. I screamed as my other mates wrung an orgasm from my abused body. That pushed him over the edge, his hot seed sliding down my throat.

They all kissed and held me in turns as we came down from the high of amazing sex. Warmth and love thrummed in our bonds. I'd never felt more content in my life.

"Did you have fun?" Marlow asked as I finally stood, "Ready to become Queen of the Occident Dragons?"

"Ready as I'll ever be." I said with a grin as I moved into the bathroom. Our official coronation was in two hours. Regardless of what had happened with Adam, I was ready to become Queen. The Dragon Clans of the Occident needed me, and I was finally ready to meet my destiny.

***

I COULD HEAR the bustling of the crowd from my place inside. Unlike our other ceremonies, all coronations took place outside. My Dragon would need the space as I came into my full power.

"Don't get nervous on me now." I muttered to myself.

"Talking to yourself is a bad sign." Mateo's voice had me turning around excitedly. I rushed to him, throwing my arms around him, "It's good to see you, Fallon."

"Are you... back?" I wasn't sure how to ask for an update on Hambridge.

He grinned, "Lady Vanessa is doing well ruling over Clan Hambridge. I won't be returning with her."

"You did it." I breathed, "Thank you."

"I'm sorry I missed... everything." I could tell from the worry in his eyes that he'd heard about Adam.

"You're here now. That's good enough." I hugged him tightly. "It's almost time."

"You're going to make a wonderful Queen. No one has ever doubted that." He reassured me, "I'll be right in front if you need me."

Once he left, I smoothed the red ballgown I wore down. It had been made to mimic my scales in color. I picked at one of the shimmering jewels that had been sewn on. A representative of every Clan that belonged to me was waiting outside, including Marlow's mother. I was nervous, it was rare for the Clans to gather in this way. My mother's funeral had been an exception, but I'd been to overcome by grief to pay much attention to our people.

My mates arrived next, dressed in full suits, each of them looking refined and delicious. Like the Kings they truly were. I tried not to drool as Archer, grabbed my chin, "It's time to become a Queen, Fallon."

I nodded, allowing him, Bain, and Marlow to step outside first. A hush fell over the crowd as I heard Lady Mika say, "Introducing, the mates of Princess Fallon. Prince Archer Dabel, Marlow Faelor, and Bainbridge Abasom." They stepped out of my sight, but claps accompanied each of their names. "And finally, Princess Fallon Eyre." I stepped out, looking at a sea of people. Every Dragon in Mercy Valley was in attendance, cheering and clapping as I made my way to stand next to Mika. "Today we are gathered here, in the shadows of tragedy, to raise Fallon to the Queen of the Occident Dragons." She stepped toward me, producing the crown I'd seen my mother wear a handful of times. Twisted gold, three rubies sparkling at its peak. "It is my honor not only to crown her as Queen, but to be the first to swear my loyalty to her name." She dropped to the ground, a fist over her heart, "I acknowledge, Fallon Agana Eyre, as my Queen."

My beast awoke at her words, our power flooding through my body. My wings burst free as another woman stepped forward, "I acknowledge, Fallon Agana Eyre, as my Queen." The round, brunette woman gave me a small wink, and I instantly knew who she was. Marlow's mother, Lady Faelor. With each Clan, I felt my power unlock, fire rolled in my stomach. My beast was on edge as a final man stepped forward, "I acknowledge, Fallon Agana Eyre, as my Queen." His accent was thick, but whatever magic governed shifters did not care. My beast burst through my skin, shifting into our Dragon form in an instant. Blue and purple fire streamed from my throat into the sky above us. Behind me, my mates had all transformed, their own streams of fire joining mine. Through my beast's eyes I watched as every person kneeled. "All hail, Queen Fallon, King Archer, King Marlow, and King Bain. May their rule be blessed and long." The voices were one to my beast's ears, words she did not care to hear or acknowledge as she lifted up soaring over the crowd. Our body had gotten larger, still smaller than any of my mates, but our power shimmered over our scales.

I was finally Queen of the Occydent Dragons. My mates were by my side. As we sailed toward the stars, our Clan joined us, roars of celebration echoing in the hilltops. I felt close to my mother as I led my people into flight. I was her legacy, and I would continue her work to bring peace to all Shifters.

"There's no reason to be nervous, Fallon. She's already accepted you as Queen. I have no doubt that she'll adore you." Marlow said as we walked down to breakfast.

I rolled my eyes. Of course, he didn't understand. Just because my meeting with Queen Phaedra had gone well didn't mean his mother would like me as well. Not to even consider his sister, whom I hadn't even seen yesterday.

Mateo was already in the dining room, pouring orange juice into each cup as we entered. At the far end of the table sat Marlow's mother; to her right, a younger woman with a shock of bright blonde hair sat, looking bored. His mother beamed as we entered, standing and rushing to hug her son. "I hate that I'm not going to see ye every day." She cried, "My perfect boy." When she turned toward me, I was prepared for scorn, but instead she wrapped me in a warm hug. "And look at yer perfect lil mate. So pretty!"

"Thank you, Lady-" I began to say.

"Ah, ah. None of that now. Yer one of me daughters now. Call me Ma or Petunia." She insisted.

"You're too kind, Petunia," I said, taking a seat at the other end of the table. Bain had slipped in and taken his seat to my left while she had greeted us.

"This is my daughter, Marnie." She introduced, "You'll have to ignore her, she's in her teen rebel phase."

"Mother." Marnie snapped, "Sorry, Queen Fallon. She can be a bit much."

"Just Fallon is fine, Marnie. We are family after all." I said.

"Don't remind me that my brother has sex now." She gagged, "But it's good to have another girl to talk to."

After that, we settled into a comfortable conversation. Archer arrived with plates of food he had prepared. Petunia couldn't help but fawn over being served by her King.

"I'm stuffed." I groaned. I'd scarfed down five pancakes and probably half a pound of bacon as we had talked. With more power, my beast was starving, but now I felt like I might explode. "I think I'm going to go for a run. Does anyone want to join me?"

Bain stood with me, "I will."

"Ma and Marnie are flying out before lunch. I'm going to stay here." Marlow said, pressing a kiss to my cheek.

I turned to them, "It was so good to meet you. You and your family are welcome in our home anytime you'd like to make the flight."

Petunia grinned, standing to wrap me in a tight hug, "I'll be taking ye up on that offer. Marlow is me baby boy. I'll be missing him greatly."

"Ma." My mate groaned, but he was smiling as he pressed a kiss to my head, "I'll see you later, pet. Enjoy yer run."

Archer had already disappeared into the office upstairs; some business he needed to handle for the restaurants he still owned. So Bain and I headed out on our own. The sun shone brightly overhead as we pounded the ground. One of my favorite parts of living so deep into the mountains was the many trails that surrounded our home. We had chosen one at random, running in silence for the most part. I stopped to admire some flowers that were freshly blooming. Their bright blue petals reminding me of Bain's eyes. As I turned to show him, I found myself alone. The forest around me was silent. My beast awoke as the hairs on the back of my neck stood on end. I didn't call out, just turned in a circle, glancing around for any sign of my mate.

"If you want him alive, you're going to cooperate with me." Adam's voice echoed around me.

"Show yourself, coward." I snapped. He came from my left, dragging a silver net behind him. Bain was trapped, rage sparkling in his eyes. I cringed as I truly saw the damage I'd done to Adam's face for the first time. His eyebrows were gone, the skin on his forehead and left cheek completely melted away. It was something out of a horror movie, but I didn't care. *Stay calm. I have a plan.* I whispered through our bond. "What Adam? Failing to kill me twice wasn't enough. You've got to try again?" I said, a hand on my hip. I channeled every ounce of the party girl I'd been before he had killed my mother. "I wonder if the real reason you want to be King so bad is because you're compensating." I made a pointed look toward his crotch, "Well with your face now, no woman would want you anyway. Even a mate."

"I'm going to rip the power of the Queen from your bones while you're still alive." Adam screeched, unable to control his rage. I caught him around the middle, slamming him down on the ground. My beast had already risen to the surface, readying our fire to burn him to ash.

"You will die as nothing but dirt under my boot, just like you lived as dirt under my mother's." I unleashed myself then, talons and fire and rage. I channeled every second of grief I'd experienced for the last nine months into ending my Uncle. When I was done, not a single scrap of Adam Eyre remained. I wouldn't stop there either; his name would be wiped out of the family tree. I would ensure no one dared to speak of him for centuries to come.

I dropped to my knees as every ounce of fight was sapped from my body. *It is done.* My beast whispered before returning to the back of my mind. I had done it. I had finally avenged my mother's death. Yet as Bain wrapped his arms around me, it wasn't joy I felt, but bone deep exhaustion.

"You did amazing, Fal. It's over. It's finally over. You're safe." Bain swept me into his arms, rushing us back to the house.

Marlow and Archer met us at the door, questions buzzing, but it was all white noise to me. My beast had drained my energy completely with her show of power. I drifted into a dreamless sleep.

***

I SAT STRAIGHT UP in bed, tossing the blankets that had been tucked around me off. Before I could open the door, Archer spoke from the corner of the room, "It was real. He's gone."

"How did you know-" I started to ask.

"I've got a direct line into your brain." He pointed out, "Now get back in bed. You might feel better, but your power has been drained."

"I'm not tired." I crossed my arms over my chest.

"I can fix that." He rumbled, wrapping a hand around my throat. "On the bed on your stomach, clothes off." I considered disobeying for a moment, but he slapped my ass, propelling me into motion. I laid down, spreading my legs wide, expecting him to play with me. Instead, Archer straddled my hips, digging his fingers into the muscles of my back. I groaned as he massaged all of the tension from my body. He even massaged my glutes, carefully avoiding any touches that were too intimate. Even so, I squirmed, my body heating with lust. I wiggled under him, lifting my hips slightly as he rubbed down my thighs. He slapped each of my ass cheeks, leaving them stinging. "It's Bain's turn with you tonight. I want to make sure you're relaxed first."

I turned my head, "Bain's turn?"

"We talked. While we love having you all together, each of us wants to have time alone with you as well. Three nights a week, you'll have just one of us in your bed. The rest, we'll share." He explained as he rubbed my feet, "He'll be here in a minute. I happen to know his plan, so I thought I'd get you ready for him." Anticipation heated my skin even more. Archer pulled away, leaning down to kiss me soundly, "Be a good girl, Fallon."

"Never, Archer." I smiled as he slapped my ass one last time before leaving the room. Seconds later, Bain stepped in, a bag thrown over his shoulder.

He sat the bag at the end of the bed, and pulled me into his arms. "I'm so glad you're okay."

"I'm good, Bain." I purred as I ran my hands under his shirt, feeling the muscles of his abs contract as I touched them. "Archer said you have something planned tonight?"

He cleared his throat, "If you're willing to trust me, yes."

"I trust you with my life." I confirmed, "I am yours to use tonight, Bainbridge." His pupils blew wide with lust, as he fumbled to unzip the bag he'd brought with him. He produced a silk black blindfold from the depths, placing it over my eyes. A thrill ran through me as he pressed something between my lips, I ran my tongue over it realizing it was a ball gag. He laid me back, lifting my legs in the air. I felt rope around my ankles before I was spread wide open. He stopped touching me for a long moment, and I whined, unsure where he had gone.

"I'm right here, angel." He murmured close to my ear, "I love rope, and I've been dying to see you all tied for me." He pinched one of my nipples before clamping something over it, immediately doing the next one. Next, my wrists were lifted, tied above my head. My pussy was dripping when he finally ran a finger between my folds. I was completely at his mercy, and it thrilled me to no end. I loved seeing a new side of my mate. When something hard pressed against my ass, I tensed slightly, causing a sharp slap against my exposed pussy. I relaxed instantly, allowing him to fill my ass. "I'm going to fuck you now, but you aren't allowed to cum until I say." I whined as he slowly pressed inside me. He fucked me slowly at first, ensuring every stroke rubbed over my g spot. Eventually, he lost control, slamming into me with enough power to make me scream around the gag. My entire body shook from holding off my building orgasm, and I cried from the effort. "Cum right now, Fallon. Cum on your mates cock." Bain commanded.

I fell apart instantly, screaming and crying as he fucked me through my orgasm. He followed me into the pleasure, hot cum painting my insides. He stayed inside me through the aftershocks. The ripped the ball gag away first, capturing my lips with his, "My perfect mate." He whispered, before untying me, "I love you so much."

"I love you too." I said as I snuggled into his side. My mates were perfect for me, hand-picked by whatever God had created the Shifters. I had no doubts about that now that I had bonded with them. Together, we would protect Mercy Valley and all the Dragon Clans. A new day was dawning, and I could not wait to meet it. I was utterly drained again, so it was easy to drift off to sleep, visions of the future filling my dreams.

EPILOGUE

SIX MONTHS LATER

"JUST CLOSE THE CASE, Conri. It's been handled." I said into the phone as Archer drove.

"Fallon… We need more answers than this. Can you at least give me a name?" Conri begged, "It's been over a year since she died now. I have to write a final report before I close the case."

I sighed. We'd been having this same conversation for weeks. Conri would call and insist that I tell him the details of who killed my mother. I just told him it was taken care of. "Fine. Put in your report that it was a nobody Dragon and was handled by the Mercy Valley Clan."

There was a pregnant pause, "Is that true?"

"It's the closest thing you're going to get," I said, before I hung up the phone.

"He's truly relentless," Archer said.

"Like a dog with a bone," Marlow added.

We all fell into laughter at that. The wolf shifters had been unsettled lately. I was sure it had something to do with Radley's sudden retirement from politics, but I hadn't asked too many questions. I'd been too focused on the Clans and solidifying our rule to worry about the other shifters in Mercy Valley. That was changing today.

"Turn left. The cottage they're renting is right up here." I directed. Marlow had decided to run for Mayor. It probably wasn't legal, considering he hadn't been an American citizen for long, but the rules of Mercy Valley didn't obey the rules of... well, anyone but us. It had been a close race, but he had won.

"Explain what we're doing again?" Bain asked.

"We're greeting the new shifters that just moved into town," I explained. "Marlow is technically responsible for it, but with our role in Mercy Valley, I think we should all greet them."

"She really just wants to go see Mika and baby Dewey." Archer pointed out, "She knows we've got to drive by there on the way back home."

"Don't tell me you have baby fever." Bain sounded genuinely concerned.

"No! No. We agreed we wouldn't even consider hatchlings for at least five years." I said.

"She definitely has baby fever." Marlow mock whispered, "But we have the rest of our lives together for that." He was right, of course. Ever since Dewey had hatched, I'd been completely enamored. Dragon babies stayed in their Dragon forms for the first year of their lives, and he was the cutest little blue Dragon I'd ever seen. A part of me did want hatchlings, but I was young. I wanted more time with my mates before we took that step.

"We're here." Archer nudged me, pointing to the small yellow cottage. It was nestled just outside of any shifter territory. Several houses like it were scattered around Mercy Valley, allowing Shifters who needed to get away a place to fly under the radar. It also allowed them to decide if they wanted to join any of the Shifter packs in town.

We approached the house as a group. Bain carried a welcome basket with gift cards, snacks, and a Mercy Valley t-shirt. I knocked, painting a bright smile onto my face. An older woman opened the door cautiously, "How can I help you?"

"Hello! I'm Fallon Eyre, I'm the Mayor's wife and Queen of the Occydent Dragons. We wanted to welcome you and your family to Mercy Valley." I said, as Bain offered her the gift basket.

Her eyes widened slightly, as she bowed her head, "It's an honor to meet you. I'm Amaris King. Come in, come in." She moved to the side, allowing us into her small home. "This is my daughter in law, Vasilisa King," She motioned to a younger ginger woman, who gave us a small nod. "And my granddaughter, Antaliya King." The girl was taller than me by several inches, with wide hips and curves I would die for. Her strawberry-blonde hair was swept back from her face, revealing a long, elegant neck.

Antaliya grinned, "It's nice to meet someone closer to my age." Her smile was bright, green eyes sparking as she shook my hand. "I know y'all are Dragon shifters, and I'm a Wolf Shifter, but I really hope we can be friends."

Her energy was infectious, "I'd love that. We're so happy to have you in Mercy Valley. Let me introduce you to my mates. Archer Dabel, Bain Abasom, and finally, your Mayor Marlow Faelor."

"Three mates?" Antaliya whispered, "Damn girl... You have to be tired at the end of the day."

I laughed, "I keep them on their toes."

"Give me your number. We have to get brunch soon. I need details." She handed me her phone, allowing me to put in my number, "Just call me Taliya, by the way or Tali. I prefer it."

We chatted for a long while, as Marlow talked to her grandmother about the town. When it was time to go, she wrapped me in a big hug, "I never make friends easily. Thanks for coming up here to meet us."

"I'm sure you're going to find lots of friends in Mercy Valley." I responded.

I heard her whispered, "I hope so." as I walked away.

We all piled back in the car, "Okay... Ye noticed the power

coming off that girl, right?" Marlow asked as we drove off. "It was damn near suffocating."

"Have the wolf shifters met her yet?" Archer asked.

I shrugged, "She seems nice. I'm sure they'll be happy here." I had noticed the power rolling off of her, similar to mine in a strange way, but it had only made me more fond of her.

***

"My mom told me to tell you hello." Marlow groaned as he climbed into bed. "She also asked me three times when she can expect little Fallon's to be running around."

"Why is that on everyone's minds so much today?" I asked, with a laugh. "She's going to be disappointed that no little Marlow's will be terrorizing the house anytime soon."

"She'll live." He said, pressing a kiss to my cheek. "Plus, I'd much rather practice." He gripped my hips, lifting my body until my naked pussy was inches from his face, "What do you say?"

"Please sir." I moaned out as he licked my clit. My hips stuttered, grinding against his beard as he rushed me to my first orgasm. As soon as my body tensed, he yanked me down his body, dropping me onto his cock unceremoniously. I rode him, as his hand wrapped around my throat, choking me as he slammed his hips into me. His orgasm was quick, but I rode him through the first one, pumping until he was hard again. When he sat up, turning me over and pressing my face into the bed I expected him to keep fucking me.

Instead, he kissed up my spine, "I never expected to be so blessed." He muttered into my ear. "My perfect pet, full of my cum and so desperate for more. Such a naughty girl."

I arched my ass up, but instead of giving me what I wanted he rained smacks down. Turning my ass red hot in seconds. Then he parted my cheeks, prodding my ass, "I think I'll take you here instead.

Make you cum just from fucking your little ass." I groaned, pressing into his finger. He pulled away, replacing it with his cock. I hissed at the stretch, not as prepared as usual. He spanked me again, "This is punishment, pet. You shouldn't tease me, if you don't want all the consequences."

He spanked and fucked me until tears were running down my face. "Please, please, please, please."

"Poor little pet. Can't you cum from just my cock deep in your ass?" Marlow taunted. His hand drifted lower, slapping against my swollen pussy, "How about this?" He kept fucking my ass and slapping a hand over my pussy. The overstimulation was too much, and I screamed as an orgasm finally raced down my spine. Marlow had no mercy, though. He fucked my ass long after my orgasm was over, until he roared his own deep inside me. When he finally pulled out, he spread my cheeks apart obscenely, "Look at that. My mate with both holes swollen and dripping with my seed." He licked along my clit, and I shook, trying to get away. "One more Fallon." He growled against me, as he forced a third orgasm from my wrecked body. I was sobbing as he gathered me into his arms, but the moment he kissed my head any pain I'd felt melted away.

My mates took care of me in every way that I needed, even the hard ones. While losing my mother had been one of the hardest times in my life, I'd come out the other side with a life I had never dreamed of before. As I laid down, curled against Marlow's chest I couldn't imagine a better world to live in. Mercy Valley had it's Queen and Three Kings, but far more importantly it had Fallon Eyre, Archer Dabel, Marlow Faelor, and Bain Abasom protecting it until the end of their days.

Acknowledgments

Fallon's story was a special one for me to write. My own journey with grief has been long, as anyone who has lost a parent can tell you, it is completely devasting. I hope you have found some solace in her story. If you are struggling with grief or depression, please reach out for help. I promise there are people who love you.

Any chance I get to practice gratitude I try to, because I have so much to be thankful for. First and foremost, I want to thank my lovely husband, Tyler. Who held my hand through every stage of grief. Eight years later, and you still support me in unexpected ways. Your dedication to my writing career reviles my own. I love you so much.

Of course, the Cantrell Clan, always get a shoutout. My family may be small, but we make up for it with big personalities.

To Leah and Larissa. The ladies who ensure my art is gorgeous, my socials run smoothly, and that I haven't totally lost my mind on this indie author journey.

To Cantrell's Chaotic Corner, an epic ARC Team. Every one of you push me to make my next book even greater. Thank you!

And most importantly, to you. The reader. Every word of mine that you read pushes me forward, I hope you founds bits of yourself in the pages of this story.

ABOUT THE AUTHOR

Taila Cantrell can be found lurking in the mountains of East Tennessee with her husband. Whether she's at her day job, wrangling the feral blue-collar men, tucked into a local bookstore, or at home curled up with her many cats and two pups, she's always plotting the next story. Her readers can look forward to many genres from fantasy romance to poetry to murder mysteries there is no story Taila isn't willing to give her voice to.

In every story, Taila blends spellbinding romance with trauma, chaos, and hope. Her books remind readers that even in the darkest moments, the heart still remembers how to burn bright.

ALSO BY TAILA CANTRELL

The Reclaiming Wonderland Series

Code Red

Code White: Frosted Wonderland

Blue Dreams

Emerald Knights (Coming May 2026)

The Austral Witches:

Primal Echoes

One Bloody Night

Two Shadowed Hearts

Three Little Doves

Four Twisted Dreams

Five Burnt Offerings (Coming June 2026)

Mercy Valley:

Wing of the Dragon

Howl of the Wolf (Coming Soon)

The Tides of Desire Trilogy w/Allena Scott

A Tide of Secrets and Storms

A Tide of Silver and Sin

A Tide of Smoke and Sirens (coming August 2026)

Standalones

Ink and Chaos: A Poetry Collection

www.ingramcontent.com/pod-product-compliance
Lightning Source LLC
Chambersburg PA
CBHW051456050726
47593CB00005B/2091